CHUPACABRA
AND THE ROSWELL UFO

RUDOLFO ANAYA

University of New Mexico Press o Albuquerque

Library of Congress Cataloging-in-Publication Data
Anaya, Rudolfo A.
ChupaCabra and the Roswell UFO / Rudolfo Anaya.
p. cm.
Summary: Folklorist Rosa Medina investigates a purported
government agency that is cloning a monster—a combination of
ChupaCabras and aliens—intended to take over the world.
ISBN 978-0-8263-4469-4 (CLOTH : ALK. PAPER)
1. Chupacabras—Fiction. 2. Extraterrestrial beings—Fiction.
3. Cloning—Fiction. 4. Conspiracies—Fiction.
5. Hispanic Americans—Fiction. 6. Roswell (N.M.)—Fiction. I. Title.
PZ7.A5186CH 2008
2008011749

Book and jacket design and type composition by Kathleen Sparkes.
Jacket illustration by Mary Sundstrom
This book was composed using Palatino OTF 10.5/14.5; 25P3.
Display type is Roadkill.

CHUPACABRA AND THE ROSWELL UFO

CHAPTER 1

Rosa Medina woke with a start.
She sat up in bed and glanced at the clock: 2:00 a.m. Through the window wafted the warm air of a Los Angeles spring night. A sultriness covered the city like a blanket of wet duck feathers.

She lay back down and listened. There it was again, the sound that had awakened her. Her heart beat faster; a shot of adrenaline curled in her stomach.

Someone was in her apartment. Someone or something was moving in the dark.

Rosa reached for the phone. Why hadn't she taken Bobby's advice and enrolled in the gun training course he had suggested?

You must keep a pistol in your apartment, he had insisted.

Why? she asked.

He hesitated. She pressed him for an answer.

For protection, he said.

Rosa wished she had listened. A pistol in her hand would make her feel safer. But she abhorred the idea of keeping a gun. Sooner or later guns went off and people got hurt.

"Damn," she whispered. The phone was dead, the wires probably cut, and her cell phone was in her purse in the living room.

She jumped out of bed and locked the bedroom door. Pressing against it she heard a shuffling sound. The same sound she had heard the ChupaCabra make aboard the cruise ship. The hair on the back of her neck bristled. She sniffed the air. The stench in the air was the sulfurous smell of ChupaCabra.

Is this what Bobby had alluded to? The ChupaCabra would return for its revenge. It had not died when the cruise ship went down in flames!

A loud bang at the door made Rosa jump back.

It was here! The ChupaCabra had found her!

The blow splintered the door. The next blow would rip the door open.

Turn on the light! No, it was better to face the beast in the dark. Call for help? No one would hear, and if they did, it would be too late. She had seen the ChupaCabra kill. Its attack was swift and deadly. Its fangs latched onto a victim's skull and destroyed the brain.

The baseball bat! She had been playing softball with a group of women from the barrio. East L.A. Chicanas, Hijas de Malinche they called themselves. All except Rosa were two-hundred-pound mujeres out to lose weight, pounds they quickly put back on after playing by drinking beer and eating burritos and deep-fried tacos.

Rosa reached for the bat, held it over her head, and waited. The expected blow came, the door flew open, and in rushed the creature, its eyes glowing red.

Rosa swung; the bat cracked against the ChupaCabra's head.

"Bishh!" It cried in pain.

She swung again and the bat hit the beast square between the eyes. It fell back into the dark hallway, howling in pain. Rosa heard it crashing through the furniture and then the front door slammed shut.

She rushed to the window in time to see the figure of a man

jump into a waiting car. Tires squealed as the dark car jumped forward and sped away into the night.

Rosa flipped on the lights and rushed to secure the front door. She propped a chair under the doorknob and tested it. The chair would hold the door against a tough intruder—but not against a ChupaCabra.

Breathing a sigh of relief, and trembling from the confrontation, she grabbed her purse and returned to the bedroom.

The ChupaCabra had not come to break into her home, a man had. She paused at the door. Blood splattered the doorframe. On the floor lay the green mask the attacker had used—red eyes, horns, a mouth with large sharp teeth, devil-like. Ugly enough to scare anyone in the dark. Whoever broke into her apartment had come to harm her.

Who? Why?

Still shaken by the ordeal, she fished her cell phone out of her purse and called Bobby.

"Someone just broke into my apartment," she said as calmly as possible. "Can you come—"

Secure the apartment, I'll be right over was his immediate answer.

Minutes later his car screeched to a stop outside. Rosa pulled the chair away and opened the door. Bobby Mejía, LAPD detective, rushed in, service revolver in hand.

"You all right?" he asked, surveying the room.

Rosa nodded. "He's gone."

"How many?"

"Just one. A car was waiting outside—"

"Let me look anyway," he replied and made his way down the hall into the bedroom. He checked the bathroom and closet. "All clear. You sure you're okay?"

"Scared, but alive."

"There's blood on the door."

"I hit him with a bat."

Bobby nodded. "He probably won't come back. And this?" He picked up the mask the attacker had used.

"The mask he was wearing. A ChupaCabra mask."

Bobby frowned. He had been with Rosa aboard the cruise ship that was delivering a multimillion drug shipment into L.A. Together they had faced the ChupaCabra. As it neared L.A., the ship caught fire and burned. The dope, the drug smugglers, and the monster were destroyed. Or so they thought. The newspapers, TV news, and the Internet had publicized Rosa's role in the story; the drug cartel knew she was responsible for its loss.

"You were right," Rosa said. "I should have bought a gun."

"Looks like you did all right with the bat." Bobby forced a smile. His cop instinct told him Rosa was not safe. Whoever broke in had come to hurt her.

"What's this?" He picked up a crumpled sheet of paper.

"He must have dropped it," Rosa said.

"It's a ticket stub from the Roswell UFO Museum. Does it mean anything to you?"

Rosa shook her head.

"I'll call the station—"

"Why?"

"We have to analyze this blood sample for DNA, check where the mask was bought, do a thorough search of the premises—"

Rosa sighed. "It will be in the papers again . . . another ChupaCabra scare. Reporters hounding me. . . . Just when I was getting my life back . . ."

Her voice broke; Bobby pulled her close. "Shh. I understand. It's okay. We can handle this."

CHAPTER 2

No sooner had Bobby left than her cell phone rang.

"Rosa. This is Ed."

"Ed?" Rosa replied.

"From high school. Remember? The cat."

Rosa vaguely remembered Ed. He had transferred to Santa Fe High during her senior year. He didn't seem to make many friends. He always seemed engrossed in a science project. He predicted the Santa Fe River would die because housing projects were taking all its water. The science teacher loved him until he dissected a cat to show organ similarity between cats and humans.

Rosa had heard he'd gotten a degree in science from the University of New Mexico. Biology. The last she'd heard he was teaching at Eastern New Mexico University in Portales.

"I know about you and el ChupaCabra. You have to be careful, Rosa."

"Ed. Where are you?"

"I'm in Roswell. You have to come here."

"Why?"

"You're on their hit list—"

"Whose hit list?"

"They're cloning people—"

Was he drunk? Was this some kind of joke? She was in no mood for joking. But she heard fear in Ed's voice, so she calmly asked, "How did you get my number?"

"Everybody's got your number, Rosa. Don't you know? The Internet."

Yes, in the Internet age everybody's information was there, waiting to be hacked. "What are you talking about Ed?"

"The alien spaceship that crashed near Roswell. The alien autopsy. They're cloning the aliens!" His voice rose, clearly irritated.

"Go on," she said softly.

"You know, they cloned the alien. First it was the U.S. Army with all their lies! Majestic-12. That's old. Now it's C-Force. Clone Force. They froze the alien, and as soon as the technology was available, they cloned himit."

"Himit?" Rosa asked.

"It's not a *him* and it's not an *it*. It's a *himit*!" Ed laughed. Rosa considered hanging up. Bobby warned her there might be more danger. Every crazy in the world intrigued with the ChupaCabra incident had her number and knew where she lived.

But she hadn't counted on Ed calling with wild stories about cloned Roswell aliens. She was interested in myths and legends to be sure. That's why she had done years of research on ChupaCabras. She had no way of knowing she had been destined to come face-to-face with a ChupaCabra aboard the cruise ship. No way of knowing the beast would kill her graduate assistant and one of the kids she was tutoring at the community center.

Ed's warning echoed in Rosa's head. "There's danger all around. You better come, if you want to save yourself."

"Save myself from what?"

"ChupaCabras. They're cloning ChupaCabras!" Ed shouted. "I hacked their computers!"

Cloning ChupaCabras? Rosa made an effort to keep from laughing. Who in the hell would clone a ChupaCabra? How? It didn't matter. Just listening to him made her an accomplice in his fantastic story. Or was it a weird joke?

"Look, Ed—"

"I know, I know," he whispered hoarsely. "You're too busy! The whole world is too busy! Just wait till thousands of ChupaCabras are loose! Remember the movie where the dead come out of their graves? They can't be killed. They're already dead!"

Why was she listening, she asked herself. Because her academic training and interest in recording folklore had taught her to listen to the wildest stories. Behind the most improbable story often lay a grain of truth.

"They have biologists who have cloned humans. They do it for the money. C-Force took them to Puerto Rico."

"Puerto Rico?"

"They found the lost colony. C-Force used ChupaCabra DNA to mix with alien DNA."

"What lost colony?"

"The ChupaCabras. In the mountains. The U.S. Army had saved alien DNA from the '47 crash. There are clones walking around Roswell."

"But—" Rosa paused, feeling foolish for listening to the crazy story. "Alien DNA?"

"You flunked science didn't you? The DNA is all over the universe. The Big Bang spread the components all over the universe. The spark of life, God, made all those bubbling nutrients come alive. Either way, we're all related. We're all primos under the skin. It's in the DNA. C-Force has the stuff and they have the lab!"

"In Roswell?"

"Yes. The cloned ChupaCabras in Puerto Rico got loose. People began to spot some of them in their backyards. The ChupaCabras went from killing goats to people. Some uninformed police found the lab and the press got hold of the bust, so C-Force had to get out of Puerto Rico. Moved back to Roswell. The '47 UFO had landed here. The alien autopsy is on film! There were alien guts, blood, and skin spread all over the crash site. The government boys picked up everything. Froze it until the cloning technology came along. It's basic science. Textbook stuff. Remember *Jurassic Park*? C-Force didn't need the DNA in the blood of a mosquito. They had the real stuff!"

"But—" Rosa cut in.

"The ChupaCabra? Same thing. Skin samples. The ChupaCabra left its DNA behind. Left its saliva on your two friends it killed."

Rosa felt a chill. So Ed knew about José and Chuco. Why not? The news media had publicized their deaths. But why tell her the ChupaCabra left saliva on its victims? The image was gross, but true, she supposed. Didn't every toothed animal that bit into its victims leave saliva behind?

"But who would gather—" She stopped. The idea of someone gathering ChupaCabra saliva was more than her queasy stomach could take. "Ed, I don't have time—"

"You have to make time, Rosa! They're out to get you! There's a conspiracy, Rosa. C-Force controls the clones. They want what you have."

"What?"

"Listen," Ed interrupted.

Rosa listened, but Ed's breathing was the only thing she heard. Even his breath carried a sense of fear.

"Ed? Are you there?"

"I'm standing across the street from the UFO Museum. Roswell's cash cow. If the city fathers only knew."

"Ed, how do you know about C-Force?" Rosa asked. What her old classmate was proposing was insane. But now she was part of his story, part of his conspiracy, and like any good researcher she had to ask her informant where he got his information.

"I got past their firewall," Ed answered. "Hacked their computers. I know enough to put two and two together—listen!"

Rosa pressed the phone against her ear. There it was! The sound she had heard the ChupaCabra make aboard the cruise ship. A high screeching cry. She could almost smell the sulfurous stench that accompanied the beast.

"Oh God!" Ed shouted. "It's too late!"

Rosa heard his cry of terror, then something like flesh being torn apart. There was a final, horrible scream and the phone went dead.

CHAPTER 3

Bobby, Leo, and Mousey arrived early to say good-bye. Rosa didn't pack much into her Honda. Clothes, her books and research papers, her guitar, and a small statue of the Virgin from her altar.

The attack had made her decide to head for Santa Fe sooner than she had planned. Bobby had insisted. In so many words he let her know L.A. wasn't safe for her. Being chased by a ChupaCabra aboard the cruise ship had been an ordeal that still brought nightmares. She had missed her period. The clinic doctor examined her and said it was stress. She needed rest. And the recent attack had convinced her to go on leave. She applied for leave from the university and it was granted. Both colleagues and the administration knew what she had been through.

After the violent end to her phone call with Ed, Rosa had called Bobby and told him Ed's story. He immediately checked with the Roswell police. The report was unsettling.

"The Roswell chief of police said an unidentified male had been found dead near the UFO Museum. Savagely beaten to death."

"A ChupaCabra," Rosa said.

What could Bobby say. He had been with Rosa on the cruise ship. He had looked into the burning red eyes of the beast. He had seen it kill the ship doctor. Part of his analytical detective mind still wanted to believe ChupaCabras were only a figment of imagination, a story told by old people in the barrios. But he had been there.

"Why unidentified?" asked Rosa.

"No driver's license, no social security card—"

"But he taught at Eastern; can that be traced?"

Bobby shrugged. "I'll keep looking into it."

"Was Ed onto something?" Rosa mused. "There have been ChupaCabra sightings in Puerto Rico, Mexico, here in L.A., and dozens of other places. Now Roswell. And remember the UFO story? An alien UFO supposedly crashed there in 1947. An alien was found in the wreckage, and later an autopsy was performed. I've seen the videotape of the autopsy. The army insisted it was a weather balloon that crashed, not a UFO. They put a lid on any information that had to do with the crash."

"The lid must still be tight. The police chief was definitely reluctant."

"A government conspiracy? That's what the believers in extra-terrestrial beings claim. But cloned aliens? And cloned Chupa-Cabras? I feel like I'm slipping into a science fiction time warp."

"You're not," Bobby insisted, holding her. "You're in real time. I agree with the doctor—you've been through a lot. You need rest. I only wish I was going with you."

"I do too," she said. In his embrace she felt secure. His love and reassuring presence had helped her through the ordeal.

"Hey, profe!" Leo called as she and Mousey entered noisily. "Got the car all packed. Oooh, amorcitos. Que romantic."

Mousey pouted. "I feel sad."

Rosa reached out to the two students she had tutored at Self Help. Chuco was dead and Indio had fled to New Mexico to live with his uncle. That would be Rosa's first stop: the Navajo reservation. She had called Indio and told him she would stop by on her way to Santa Fe.

"Don't be sad. You can come see me this summer. Soon as I'm settled you come with Bobby—"

"Hey! Great!" Mousey exclaimed. "I want to see real cowboys!"

"Cállate!" Leo punched his shoulder. "The profe needs rest. We're not going to bother her."

"But I've never been to New Mexico. I want to see Indio—"

"Look, pendejo, we're here to say good-bye, not to make plans to go to New Mexico. You don't even know where the state is."

"I do," Mousey replied. "It's near Utah. Ain't it, profe?"

Rosa laughed. "Yes, it's near Utah. And you will come. We'll all go together and visit Indio." She turned to Bobby. "I'm ready."

"Anything else to pack?"

"My backpack."

"I got it," Leo said. "Come on, Mousey, let's boogey." She grabbed him and led him outside.

Rosa looked around the apartment. Already it seemed empty.

"I have a strange feeling," she whispered. "A premonition—"

Bobby held her and looked into her eyes. "You'll be okay. Family and rest will be good for you. Hey, the woman who stood up to a ChupaCabra can handle anything."

Rosa kissed him. She hadn't planned to fall in love. She had been busy with her career when suddenly there he was, and what surprised her more was that she felt good about it. She knew their love was strong. It would survive even this parting.

"You're good for me . . . good to me. I only wish—"

"Time to be together. That will happen, I promise you. Right now you need a break."

"And time to do research," Rosa added.

"Hey, you're not thinking of going to Roswell are you?"

"I admit, Ed's story intrigued me."

Bobby shook his head. "He was probably on something. The

homeless die every day on the streets. I'm sure Roswell is no different. Look, you don't owe him anything. You hadn't seen him in years. People get to the bottom and they reach out in strange ways."

That was it, Rosa thought. Ed had reached out to her. He knew about her ChupaCabra experience. He insisted the monster was being cloned. Was he delusional? Drunk? On drugs? Maybe, but there was something about his wild story that intrigued her. Following the ChupaCabra into the jungles of Mexico had taught her the improbable can come true, and reality can turn deadly.

"Yes, you're right," she said. "Now, I better hit the road. I want to be at Indio's place before sunset."

They walked outside into a hazy L.A. morning. Leo and Mousey stood near the car. Leo cried and embraced Rosa. "You're the best teacher we've ever had."

"Yeah, profe, the best," Mousey agreed, wiping his eyes. "Damn, it's hard to be macho!" he exclaimed.

"I'll be back," Rosa said. "You two keep up with your studies."

"We'll miss you, profe."

"I'll miss you—" she turned to Bobby. "And you."

He kissed her and held her for a moment. "We'll be okay. You take care. And get going, otherwise I'm going to have trouble being macho myself."

She reached up and wiped a tear from his cheek. "I love you," she whispered, then turned and got in the car. Bobby closed the door, winked, and she was off.

Glancing in the rearview mirror she saw them waving good-bye, friends that had become her family in L.A.

Ah well, she consoled herself, in a few weeks Bobby would take some leave time and visit her. He would meet her family and friends like Nasario García, Nash Candelaria, and Pat Mora. She wanted him to enjoy the road to Truchas and Trampas, visit John Nichols, a writer she had once interviewed for an article in Taos, and visit Frank Waters's grave site in Arroyo Seco.

She knew many of the writers in New Mexico. The state was home to authors whose stories defined the place. Not only politicians and businesspeople defined the state; writers also revealed the cultures, history, and traditions. They warned about depleted water sources as entire new populations moved into the area.

Something interrupted Rosa's thoughts. She looked in the rearview mirror and saw a black SUV following her. A Hummer— one of those gas guzzling dinosaurs driven by those in need of a status symbol. Yes, the SUV had been there for quite a while. That's what caused the unsettling feeling.

Maybe it's just my imagination, she thought. Large, black cars were in vogue. There were many on the road. She drove past Barstow and settled into the long drive across the desert. In homage to Freddie Fender she played his CDs. His songs made the lonely miles fall away, but as she neared Kingman the SUV was still pressing down on her.

"Let's see if he's really following me," Rosa whispered. She exited the interstate at a truck stop, drove behind a parked eighteen wheeler, jumped out of the car, and ran around the front of the huge truck. If she was right, she would surprise whoever was following her.

The SUV did not appear. Rosa stepped forward and looked up the road. Nothing. It had been right behind her, but suddenly it had disappeared into thin air.

CHAPTER 4

Rosa stopped in Gallup to get gas and use the bathroom. Then she turned north toward Tohatchi, eager to get to Uncle Billy's home.

Indio, whose real name was Charlie Joe Begay, had been one of her students. The last time she saw him was at Uncle Billy's hogan, where she was attacked by someone in a wolfskin. Some Navajos believed that those-who-walk-on-four-legs were witches. Yenaldooshi, the feared Skinwalkers.

As far as Rosa was concerned, the Skinwalker who attacked her was a member of the international dope smuggling cartel she had exposed. Real men dealing in brain-killing drugs. Bobby believed it was the same cartel that had sent the killer wearing the ChupaCabra mask. What did they want?

She had photos of the drug smugglers that José had taken, but she had turned those over to the L.A. County DA. All except the one photo José had taken just before he was killed: a photo of the ChupaCabra. The same photo of the monster she carried in her purse. She hadn't let anybody see it, not even Bobby. Why was she carrying it? Was she still haunted by the ChupaCabra?

Ed had said ChupaCabras were being cloned. Her analytic mind told her that was preposterous, but the part of her brain that studied legends and myths told her the monsters of the ancient past kept appearing in new guises, new masks for the ghosts from the dark primeval forests. The past was not dead.

The ancient Greeks had feared the monstrous Scylla and the whirlpool Charybdis, which sucked ships to the sea bottom. For Latinos it was la Llorona, the crying woman who haunted lakes and rivers in search of the children she murdered. These were all legends and stories woven out of people's imaginations to explain phenomena in their lives. Today's vampires and werewolves stalked the urban jungles in three-piece suits, and people went on creating stories.

Just north of Tohatchi Rosa came to the familiar dirt road that led to Uncle Billy's hogan. She turned down the gutted road, her headlights stabbing the spring night that had descended on the desert like a thick Navajo blanket.

Suddenly, just ahead, a large dog or wolf loped across her headlights and disappeared. Rosa gasped. A Skinwalker! A witch running on four legs! And right behind it a dark figure!

Rosa stopped the car and locked her door. She held her breath. The figure had disappeared. Then a loud thump on the window startled her. A dark face loomed against the glass. "Teach!" it called. "It's me, Indio!"

Rosa breathed a sigh of relief and opened the door. "Indio. Thank God—"

"Didn't mean to scare you. I've been waiting. So has Bushie." He pointed at the dog that eagerly jumped up to greet Rosa.

Rosa petted the large mongrel. "Hi . . . Bushie?"

"Uncle Billy named him. Said he's not even good for herding sheep. Come on, do you have a bag?"

"Just my backpack," Rosa replied, handing him the pack. "Thanks for being here."

"Hey, we didn't want you to get lost. You remembered the place."

"Like it was yesterday."

"Come on. You must be tired. Uncle has some mutton and red chile stew that will just melt you. He's so excited—been cleaning the camp all week."

He talked as he led Rosa toward the hogan, which was built against a large rock outcropping, a natural amphitheater of red sandstone that was warm in winter and cooled by breezes in summer. Around the side of the hogan lay the sheep pens.

"I hope you didn't go through trouble—"

"Are you kidding?" Indio interjected. "This is fun for us. We have few visitors."

"Uncle!" Indio called. "Teach is here."

Uncle Billy met them at the door of the hogan. Thin and sinewy, the sixty-year-old man cut a dignified figure. He greeted Rosa with a smile.

"Miss Rosa. Warrior Woman. Welcome to our home."

"Uncle. It is good to see you." Rosa gently touched his hand in greeting.

Years ago Uncle Billy Begay had served on the Navajo Nation council. He had worked for his people in the halls of power in Window Rock, Phoenix, Santa Fe, and Washington, D.C. Some said he was poised to be governor of the Diné people. Then his wife died unexpectedly. He quit politics and returned to his family's traditional grazing grounds.

Drugs and booze were rampant on the reservation. Uncle Billy had learned some of the healing chants as a young man, so he turned his attention to helping young Navajos by performing the traditional ceremonies. Indio had written Rosa that with his uncle's help he was clean of drugs. The ceremonies and hard work as a sheepherder had effected the cure.

"I'm clean and it feels great," Indio wrote. "This is a new life for me."

In the light cast from the open door, Rosa could see how true his words rang. Indio looked strong, full of life—a far cry from the young man who only a few months ago had struggled to escape from drug addiction.

"Come in, come in," Uncle Billy said warmly. "My casa es tu casa." He smiled. "I should say, mi hogan es tu hogan."

"It feels good to be here," Rosa said. For the first time that day a weight was lifted. The soft light of the kerosene lamps, the sweet smell of cedar burning in the stove, and the aroma of mutton stew all felt like home.

"Charlie Joe prepared this meal in your honor."

"I helped," Indio acknowledged, "but Uncle Billy is the real cook."

"I've been at it longer," Uncle Billy said. "Everything gets better with age."

They sat and ate red chile mutton stew and horno bread, which Uncle Billy confessed was the gift of a widow who lived just over the hill. He winked. "The fruit pies are also gift, but the coffee is my specialty."

Rosa stuffed herself. Navajo fare was much like the basic New Mexican food her mother would prepare at home. Hispanos, Pueblo Indians, and Navajos shared a love for red chile with meat, beans, and tortillas.

Later, sipping coffee, Uncle Billy spoke. He talked about the newspaper reports of strange lights recently spotted over Taos.

"Our neighbors who come from the sky," Uncle Billy said. "Who knows what they are. In our creation stories we say we came from the earth, but I believe there are star people. They have been coming to earth for a long time."

"Star people," Rosa said. She knew little of the Navajo creation stories. She made a mental note to do some research.

"The constellations," Uncle Billy continued. "All cultures

describe the zodiac. The Greeks named the star people. Some are monsters that eat humans."

"I don't remember a monster in the zodiac," Rosa mused.

"But we are moving into a new time," Uncle Billy said. "The end of the world as the Maya and Aztec people predicted. Maybe your ChupaCabra will appear as a new constellation. Evil people will use its power. It is a warning. Evil people desire to take over the earth. They sell the drugs that destroy our young people."

He paused and glanced at Indio. Indio nodded. He knew now that those who had sold him meth did so to gain control over him. The drugs they sold destroyed the brain. Then spirit and soul died.

Rosa listened intently. Uncle Billy was a storyteller. He talked into the night, explaining what he knew of human nature. Stories of creation involve the animal world. Eve was tempted by the serpent. In the Navajo legend the Warrior Twins kill the monster. In ancient Mexico, Quetzalcoatl appears in Aztec legend as the Plumed Serpent, half snake, half bird.

"You are tired," Uncle Billy said. "Time for you to rest."

Rosa nodded. It had been a long day. Not even Uncle Billy's strong coffee could keep her awake much longer. "I'll get some fresh air and then bed. I'm going to sleep like a baby."

"Your bed is ready," Uncle Billy said. He pointed to a small room.

"Same place I slept last time," Rosa said. "Thank you."

"Este es tu casa," Uncle Billy said. "Sleep as late as you want. Charlie and I will be up early, checking ewes that are bringing lambs into the world."

Rosa stepped outside. The cold spring air was tinged with the fragrances of sage and desert grasses. Except for the bleating of ewes in the pens and distant coyote cries, the desert silence remained pristine. Bushie came up to nuzzle her hand. He followed her as she walked up a sandy knoll. In L.A. she never saw the stars. She stood in awe at the brightness of the Milky Way—millions of suns sparkling with a vibrancy that could only mean the firmament was alive and breathing. The night sky throbbed with the true meaning of life. God had imbued the universe with spirit, and the spirit itself was God.

Rosa looked up at the constellations, the revolving dance of stars and planets. She could name a few as her vision moved across the night sky.

One particular constellation made her gasp. Was she imagining things or was the cluster of stars in the eastern horizon really in the form of a monster? No, there was no constellation named ChupaCabra. Only her imagination.

She shivered and hurried back into the hogan.

CHAPTER 5

When Rosa awoke, Uncle Billy and Indio were already out tending to the sheep. Lambing season was in full swing and they would work all day and into the night. Late spring storms could still bring snow and freezing temperatures across the Four Corners area.

Rosa dressed in jeans, an old blue shirt, and comfortable walking shoes. Her windbreaker was enough to stave off the morning chill.

Uncle Billy and Indio joined her for breakfast and invited her to stay, but they were busy and she had only dropped in for a visit. She had wanted to check on Indio. What she saw assured her he had beaten the drug addiction.

After a hearty breakfast Rosa started for Santa Fe. The simple life and the beauty of the desert reminded her of her need for inner tranquility. It would be tempting to roam all summer in the sun and open air, herding sheep by day and listening to Uncle Billy's stories at night. What healing power work and nature held. She saw health and satisfaction in Indio and his uncle. Next to them she felt pale; she felt a need to revel in the New Mexican sun.

Wordsworth and company were right, Rosa thought, the world was too much with humans. An overarching technology ruled much of the world. Would it destroy the natural world? Would the warnings about global warming come to pass? She had seen the Al Gore documentary and was determined to get involved in sounding the alarm.

But right now other concerns occupied her. Rosa was on the road toward a rendezvous with cloned aliens. Cloned ChupaCabras. The word preposterous kept rolling in her mind, but Uncle Billy's advice also rang in her thoughts. No matter how strange the phenomena of life, he said, all beings seemed to move to an understandable, eventual end. God? The Great Spirit? A conscious universe? The Tao?

The constellations do not change Uncle Billy had intoned as they sat drinking coffee, listening to cedar logs popping in the wood-burning stove, the occasional cries of coyotes in the hills, and moments later Bushie's lazy, answering howl. We humans draw imaginary lines from one star to the next, he said, then we give names to that belt of stars, the path of the planets, from Aries to Pisces. The old astrologers gave names to the creatures of the zodiac. Each culture names the images according to its legends and spiritual life. The signs of the zodiac are reflections of the inner soul of the community. The Chinese will see dragons, we see the twins who beheaded the monster, on and on it goes. The Aztecs and Mayans were great astrologers. They had their own interpretation of the star people.

Rosa had nodded. I used to see the man on the moon because that's what I read in children's books. Later, I read Aztec mythology and began to see the rabbit in the moon.

Yes, Uncle Billy had said. You are getting closer to the thoughts of your ancestors. Your Indo-Hispano people have the European father and Indian mother. The mother tells us the stars are imprinted in the soul and the soul reflects the stars. We are born of the earth, but the earth itself was once stardust. The stars affect the gravity of the earth, the gravity of the heart.

As Rosa drove she listened to conjunto music, but what really kept her company were Uncle Billy's stories.

Rosa was eager to visit friends and begin her research. She had friends in Alburquerque, Abe and Belinda, who knew the writer Ben Chavez quite well. Their insights into his life would be valuable. And she was eager to interview Tony Hillerman and Max Evans. The seminal writers were getting old. But a visit would have to wait. Instead she turned north and drove straight to Santa Fe and to her parents' home. The front door was unlocked; a note on the kitchen table explained they were visiting a sick friend. There was food in the refrigerator. Rosa had just taken out an orange juice carton when her cell phone rang.

"You don't know me," the voice said. "I'm Ed's friend. Can you meet me in front of the Lensic Theater? Right away!"

Rosa stuttered. "Who are you? Why—"

"Nadine. Ed's friend. He told you I would call, didn't he? C-Force killed him. It's important, Rosa. You don't know me, but I know all about you. You met a ChupaCabra. You're in danger. You know too much about the ChupaCabras. C-Force killed Ed. They followed you, didn't they?"

Rosa frowned. This was the second cryptic phone call she had received. First Ed, now Nadine. Whoever she was.

How does she know I was followed? Rosa wondered.

"Nadine, I appreciate your concern, but Ed didn't make sense. Now you call me, and—"

"You have to trust me, Rosa. Ed's dead. They sent a clone after him."

"How did you know I was in Santa Fe?"

"You were followed. They know everything. They know I'm calling you. We have to go to Roswell. Please come. We don't have much time."

Her voice was urgent, just like Ed's had been. But go to Roswell?

Why? Ed was dead. Going there solved nothing. Why was Ed murdered? And why had Nadine shown up?

"All right. How will I recognize you?"

"I know you," Nadine replied and the phone went dead.

Rosa shivered. She scribbled a note to her parents, slipped on her jacket, and hurried outside.

This is crazy, she kept telling herself. I just got home, I need to see my parents, I need time to write, and here I am on my way to meet someone I don't know. Why? Because Nadine said Ed had been killed by a clone? Because of the man who broke into my apartment and tried to kill me? Were these strange occurrences linked?

Her cell phone rang. Bobby's voice came through garbled. "Checked Roswell . . . Ed died same as . . . ." And just before the signal was lost ". . . be careful."

"Damn," she whispered. "I'm going to change carriers—"

She pocketed the phone and stopped in front of the theater. Across the street people wandered in and out of Dorothy's Collected Works bookstore.

Rosa looked toward the plaza. A few locals going about their business, a few tourists window-shopping.

I would love to be taking a nap in my old bed at home, she thought, waiting for Mamá to call me to red chile enchiladas, home-baked beans simmering in the crock-pot, and tortillas baking on the comal. Ah, the aroma of home-cooked food filling the kitchen and filtering throughout the house.

She walked to the corner and looked down Burro Alley. A girl waved and called, "Rosa! Behind you!"

Rosa turned as a black SUV came to a screeching stop near her. A man jumped out and grabbed her arm.

"Get in!" he ordered.

Rosa jerked back, kneed the man in the groin, and yanked free.

"Damn you!" he cried.

The girl ran up and pointed a spray can at the attacker. She let go with a squirt that blinded the man. He cursed and fell back, rubbing his eyes. She spun around and aimed the spray can at a second man who had jumped out of the car. He caught a shot of the hot pepper spray and tripped into the gutter.

"Vamos!" the girl shouted, grabbing Rosa's arm and pulling her down the alley, past startled tourists having afternoon tea at an outdoor cafe.

CHAPTER 6

The girl, whose hoarse voice on the phone had sounded world-weary, was no older then sixteen, Rosa guessed. Thin but attractive, wearing running shoes and dressed in jeans, a black sweater, and a khaki vest, the safari type with pockets. Raven black hair cut short and a black beret.

"Stop!" Rosa gasped when they had run a few blocks, down West Palace toward the plaza. "You're Nadine?"

"Yeah."

"They're not following us."

"Bullshit," Nadine responded, blowing wisps of hair from her eyes. She looked back down the street. "They don't give up."

"You blinded them. We're okay."

Rosa glanced up the street. It seemed peaceful enough. She turned and looked into Nadine's dark eyes, which held a brooding wisdom.

Nadine said, "Did you see the himit in the back seat?"

"Vaguely . . . a man."

"Not a man. Saytir. Half alien, half ChupaCabra. He never comes out of the labs. Damn, Rosa, they want you bad."

"Saytir," Rosa repeated. Half alien, half ChupaCabra. Nadine was crazy! "No such animal!" she said, shaking her head.

"Beast," Nadine said calmly, her gaze alertly studying the streets.

"Beast? What do you mean? Who is Saytir? Why did they attack me? I don't believe—"

"You don't believe? Damn Rosa, you don't know half of it. The two that attacked you are clones. Saytir's the chief honcho. He killed Ed. Ed wasn't afraid of anything, but Saytir got to him. Come on, we can talk as we walk. They hear everything."

Damn, Rosa thought. Here I go again. Two men attack me in the middle of Santa Fe and this sixteen-year-old who believes in clones rescues me. She believes Saytir is half ChupaCabra. This is preposterous! No, crazy!

"Like the Minotaur?" she said, humoring Nadine. "If there was a Minotaur in the labyrinth who was half man, half bull, then there can be a beast half alien, half ChupaCabra." She laughed.

"Exactly," Nadine answered, calm as before. "They combined alien DNA with ChupaCabra DNA."

Rosa fought a laugh. Nadine had taken the Minotaur allusion in stride. She actually believes whatever attacked me are monsters created from mixing DNA. What could be more wild?

There were legends and myths where half man, half animal creatures appeared. From the Greeks down to werewolves, vampires, and recently with the shape-shifters in Uncle Billy's stories, the Navajo Skinwalkers, the witches who walk like wolves . . . and in the stories of the old New Mexicans, brujas who turned into owls appeared. A Pueblo man once told her he saw a witch changing into a burro.

Weren't these just stories?

"The Minotaur was a story. A story told to explain certain psychological needs—"

Nadine replied, "Raaaight, sister, right. Except Saytir ain't psychological. He's real. Real evil."

"Alien clones . . . you really think . . . I don't believe—"

"Did you see their eyes?"

"Yes."

"Vacant."

"Yes."

"And their skin. Like wax?"

Rosa touched her wrist where the man had grabbed her. It was still cold, as if something dead had touched her.

"Yes."

"People say the Roswell space aliens that crashed in the desert looked like little men with big heads, big eyes, and no hair. Bullshit. What they looked like doesn't matter. C-Force found their DNA and cloned it with ChupaCabra DNA. Then they invented something like human skin to look like us. It's all basic science, Ed said. With science, everything is possible."

If it's true, thought Rosa, then the creature who grabbed me is—something out of this world.

Looking toward the plaza she suddenly realized that even Santa Fe wasn't safe.

"If they touch you, it leaves a rash," Nadine said, looking at Rosa's wrist. "Ugh, you better wash that off, or you become one of them. A himit!" She laughed, a girlish laugh. "Just kidding," she added. "Remember—if a vampire bites you, you become a vampire."

"I don't believe in vampires," Rosa said, "or clones. The UFO landed near Roswell in 1947. That's sixty years ago. These were two young men—"

"Uh-uh," Nadine interrupted. "It took that long to find the DNA they needed, then enough embryos—"

"Where did you come from?"

"Ed sent me. I followed you."

"How—"

"Mental telepathy, sister. Your thoughts are all over the place."

"You can read my thoughts?"

Nadine shrugged. "Let me have your jacket."

"What."

"Come on, just let me see it."

Rosa took off her jacket and Nadine searched the pockets.

"Your phone. They're tracing you through your phone. Better get rid of it." She dropped the cell phone in a wastebasket.

"Hey!"

"You don't need it, sister," she said and handed Rosa the jacket as they crossed the street to the plaza. "They use TSP Ed said. Terrorist Survey Program."

"Terrorist Surveillance?"

"Yeah, whatever. The government can tap all your e-mails. C-Force taps your cell phone. Be careful, they might be tapping your mind."

A street cop blew his whistle. "Hey, you're jaywalking!" he shouted.

Nadine flipped him off. "Most cops are clones," she said and laughed. "Come on, let's get a drink. Evangelos is nearby."

"You're not old enough to drink."

"I was thinking of you. Okay, we'll do coffee."

I can't believe I'm doing this, Rosa thought as they walked into a coffee shop. But the SUV was the same one that had followed her on the road from California. They knew her movements, where she would be, and they didn't come to be nice. If not for Nadine she might not have been able to fight off the two—whatever they were.

"You have what they want," Nadine explained as they sipped their cappuccinos. "You met a ChupaCabra, verdad?" She threw in Spanish for effect.

Rosa nodded.

"The cloned ChupaCabras have been appearing all over the place. You know why? Ed said the lab where they cloned ChupaCabras was in Puerto Rico, but they got loose. The first clones were nutrients—I mean, mutants. They mutated. They got picked up on ships headed for Mexico. They began to spread all over. They're all different."

She smiled a sweet smile, as if to say *I know so much.*

All this would be science fiction, Rosa thought, if I hadn't seen the beast myself.

"The lab was in Puerto Rico," Nadine continued. "That's what Ed said. The original home of the ChupaCabras. The lost colony."

"The ChupaCabra I saw went down with the ship," Rosa said, then thought, *I think.* "So why are they different?"

"Not really different. C-Force just didn't have the right DNA, or not enough of it. It was an experiment. So there are a lot of these ChupaCabras running around. Mutants, get it? But there was one whose DNA they really wanted. The one you saw on the ship. They think you have it."

"Have what?"

"Its DNA."

"Ridiculous!" Rosa scoffed. Why was she listening to this wild story? Was it because the girl had just rescued her and she owed her?

"Believe what you want, but Saytir believes you have enough of that stuff on you to kill you for it."

"Kill me? That's preposterous!"

"They tried to grab you, didn't they? This isn't a game, Rosa. They want you."

Rosa felt a chill. Something in Nadine's voice and in her eyes told Rosa the girl who had just saved her wasn't lying.

"Something you touched," Nadine suggested, "a drop of blood. Did you touch the dead boy?"

"How do you know all this?"

"It was on the Internet. The whole world knows about you, Rosa. Can I call you Rosa? You're kind of like a friend. Ed said to take care of you."

"Why? I hardly knew Ed. We went to school together . . ."

"Oh, he was in love with you, girl. Completely muy loco. You never received his messages?"

"What messages?"

"Telepathy. Ed could do it. He taught me how. That's how I found you."

Rosa drew a deep breath of air, took a sip of cappuccino, and sat back in her chair. Nadine was a beauty. She should be in school, the head cheerleader, or Juliet in the senior-class play. Nadine was also weird. The whole thing was weird, but some real things were happening. A man had attacked her in her apartment. Two strangers had just assaulted her with kidnapping in mind.

"Why aren't you in school?" she whispered.

"I'm eighteen."

"No, you're not. You're probably sixteen."

"Ah, so you can read my mind," Nadine replied, smiling. "I didn't need school. I learned from Ed."

"Where?"

"He took me in. My parents were killed when I was eight. Drunk driver. I was an orphan. I got kicked around from family to family. From Las Cruces to Taos, you name it, I've been there. I'd run away, join other homeless kids, steal, do drugs, drink a lot. Ed found me and took me in. He was like the best thing that ever happened to me."

She was lying, Rosa sensed, making up a story. Why?

"And he loved you," Nadine continued, "so now I have to protect you."

Rosa laughed. "I don't need protection."

Nadine leaned across the table. "Oh yes you do."

"I don't have ChupaCabra DNA," Rosa said. "I thank you for helping me, but I don't need protection."

"Think back. What did you touch? Ed said it could be just a drop of blood or saliva. They want it."

"To make more ChupaCabras?"

"Yes. Don't you see? The stuff is worth millions. No, Ed said billions. Dollars, Rosa. What you have is worth a fortune! Whoever clones those monsters can rule the world, and they're working on it."

She smiled and looked around for the waiter as she pocketed a package of sugar.

"For the road." She winked.

CHAPTER 7

"I ain't letting you out of my sight, Rosa. I promised Ed."

"Okay. But I have to get home. Where do you live?"

"In my car. I have a car."

"You live in your car?"

"Hey, I've lived in worse places."

"Where is it?"

"By the courthouse. Come on, I'll drive. Ed left clues for us."

"What clues?"

"You'll see. Saytir's clones aren't narcotraficantes, you know. Sure, C-Force is into drugs. For the money. We read about the dope shipment that was on the cruise ship. But C-Force also has a lot of government money. Enough to hire all the crazy scientists it needs. It's a secret project."

"A government conspiracy. And it's in Roswell?"

"C-Force is like an octopus. It's spread all over the world. The main lab is in Roswell. Our mission is to get there."

"Mission?"

"That's what Ed called it. You have a following on the Internet, you know. Numero uno ChupaCabra girl. The expert!" Nadine smiled.

Rosa shook her head. Yes, Leo and Mousey had told her almost every ChupaCabra blog on the Internet now told her story. Her frustration rose. I don't want to be the expert, she thought. Let some of the really tough Chicanas handle ChupaCabras. I just want to teach, do my research, publish my dissertation . . . but it's true, the ChupaCabra phenomenon is growing. And I'm right in the middle of it.

The sci-fi time warp she thought she had entered was real. Nadine was real, Ed had been real, and whatever conspiracy was going on in Roswell involved her. Now she had to go after Ed's clues, whatever that meant. She had to follow Nadine, or have Saytir and his thugs catch up with her and extract whatever sample of ChupaCabra DNA they thought she possessed.

The extraction, she guessed, was life threatening. They would kill her.

"What do you have in the trunk?"

Nadine's car rode low in the rear, like a lowrider's customized car. Española, lowrider capital, was just miles up the road.

"Stuff," Nadine replied.

Rosa's parents were home and overjoyed to see her. They warmly greeted Nadine. Rosa judiciously told them a few of the salient points of Nadine's story, leaving out the murder of Ed in Roswell, leaving out any mention of cloned aliens or ChupaCabras and the recent attack by Saytir's two clones.

Rosa's parents took to Nadine. During dinner she regaled them with stories of her days as an orphan and nearly had them crying. Rosa's mother pampered her, making sure Nadine ate seconds. For dessert she insisted Nadine have extra servings of natillas.

Nadine loved every minute. "These are to die for," she said. "I tasted natillas in Roswell, but they just don't know how to make them down there."

She went on telling them about her tough life on the streets, how she recovered from alcohol addiction, and how Ed had saved her. Ed was her uncle, she said. He had just died and she had to go to Roswell to make arrangements.

Rosa noted that Nadine's facts about her life kept changing. She was making up stories to hide her motives, and it was just as well. It was no time to tell her parents Ed had been killed by a ChupaCabra.

"Pobrecita. You've had such a difficult life," Rosa's mother said. "More coffee? Dessert? You're welcome to stay here tonight. I know how difficult losing your uncle must be."

"He's the only family I had left on earth," Nadine said. "Thank you, but I can't stay. I have to get to Roswell tonight."

"Terrible night to drive. The wind is starting . . ."

Rosa's mother pointed to the window. A spring wind was blowing down the Sangre de Cristo Mountains, rushing past the hills dotted with expensive homes, and moaning around the plaza. The ghostly Llorona of the Santa Fe plaza was driving everyone indoors. Twilight descended in dull, swirling orange colors. A windstorm was brewing.

"Rosa promised to help me." Nadine glanced at Rosa.

"You could start early tomorrow—"

"No, we have to be there tonight. Don't we, Rosa?"

Rosa's mother looked surprised. "But you just got here. You're tired. Don't you think—"

"She promised," Nadine insisted, looking into Rosa's eyes, a hypnotic stare.

Rosa nodded. She had already decided to follow Nadine. She owed something to Ed, and to Nadine for saving her. Besides, there was a story that involved ChupaCabras and Roswell UFO aliens. She had to go.

"Rosa said she would help me make arrangements for my uncle," Nadine repeated.

I did not promise, thought Rosa, but she knew I would go. That strong, beguiling personality has led me this far. I have to know if Ed was killed by a ChupaCabra. To date, there were no recorded ChupaCabra attacks in New Mexico. If this was one it was crucial to investigate. And just as intriguing was Nadine's wild story about Saytir and his DNA experiments.

"I did promise," Rosa said. "After all, Ed was a classmate. I feel I should do something."

Rosa's mother shrugged. "Let me talk to your father. See what he says."

"Don't worry about us, Mrs. Medina. We'll be back in a day or two. You know how it is when a family member dies. I have to be there, then I'll drive Rosa back."

"I knew all your friends. I just don't remember Ed," Rosa's mother said.

"He transferred here his senior year . . ."

"I see . . ."

"Roswell's only a few hours. It's not like we're going to Mars."

"Mars!" Nadine laughed. "Roswell's not Mars. It only feels that way!"

"I'll tell Dad," Rosa said, jumping up and excusing herself.

Rosa found him in the garage and explained the plan, which he took in stride. After all, he had raised his daughter to be self-reliant.

"Sounds hurried," he said. Then added, "She's a strange girl . . ."

"She needs help. Her uncle is dead, and I have the time . . ." Rosa's voice trailed off. Ed wasn't Nadine's uncle, and the girl could survive almost anywhere. "There might be a story there," she admitted. "Something for my research."

"Ah, I figured," her father said. "Not the ChupaCabra?"

"You've been surfing the Internet?"

He nodded. "I haven't told your mother, but you and your friend Bobby are big news on La Bloga."

Rosa kissed him. "Don't believe everything you read by the bloggers. I'll call Bobby before we leave. And thanks, Dad, thanks for everything."

"Just be careful," he cautioned.

Rosa called Bobby and told him her plans. His report was troubling. "I'm still digging into Ed's murder. As far as I can ascertain, Ed's wounds fit the ChupaCabra's MO. The skull was punctured. You have to be careful, amor."

"I will. I'll keep in touch. And you be careful. I miss you already."

"And I miss you. I'm digging up loads of stuff about Roswell on the net. It's a strange place. The whole UFO thing sounds kind of phony."

"As far as I know it's a chamber of commerce thing," Rosa suggested. "But keep digging and we can compare notes. Gotta go."

She blew him a kiss over the phone, then hurried to throw a few things into an overnight bag.

"I'm ready," she said, handing the bag to her father. "Might as well get going."

Nadine was waiting by the car, eager to start. Her nervousness had increased, although she tried not to show it.

"Be careful on the road," Rosa's father warned. "The wind is kicking up. Do you need any money?"

"No, I'm good. It's a short trip. Then I'll be around all summer bugging you."

"That kind of bugging I love," her father replied. "We'll go fishing like we used to. Up to Pecos, Taos, even try the San Juan."

"And visit family," her mother added. "So much to catch up on."

"Nadine, if you open the trunk, I'll put Rosa's bag—"

"No, Mr. Medina!" Nadine shouted, grabbing the bag. "Thanks. I'll put it in the back seat!"

Rosa's father frowned. He looked at the car's low-slung rear end and asked, "What do you have in there, a dead body?"

CHAPTER 8

"You missed the turn to get to 285," Rosa said.

Nadine smiled. "All roads lead to Roswell, and if we had time, we'd go by Santa Rosa. Land of the Golden Carp. Ed took me there. We saw the lakes, El Rito. Little river. It was summer and the trees and bushes were so green, and the little river was flowing to the Pecos River. We looked for the Golden Carp."

"See it?"

"No, we weren't lucky that day. But it's there."

Rosa knew the story. She had interviewed the writer who had written the legend of the Golden Carp. The creation story in the novel had intrigued a lot of readers, including a few PhD literature students.

"We did see Sonny Rivera's statue of the writer. It's awesome! Sonny is a genius. That's what is going to save us, sister."

"What will? Sonny? The Golden Carp?"

"All that chingadera," Nadine answered. "See, you're reading my mind. Ed said there are invisible lines running through the earth. He called them Sun Lines. The old people knew about them. Your ancestors. The Sun Lines are like, you know, spiritual. Only by knowing about them can we be saved from the mess humans have created."

"Like?"

"Like global warming. Ed had a plan to stop global warming. But the government won't put money into it. They fund genetic engineering. Why? Ed said there was a race by dictators to create clones. Create an army without hearts, without emotions. Clones can't love."

Nadine was a smart girl, but not that smart, Rosa thought. Was she just regurgitating information Ed had taught her? Or was she a child of the Internet age, ingesting only bits and pieces of information? The world had gone digital. Technology was being cloned, every day a new gadget, new chips, smaller and smaller, made from silicone and plastic, the children needed games, the military needed the latest. Wireless. All throwaway stuff.

"What was Ed to you?" Rosa asked.

"A savior. He could read a book in like five minutes. Then he'd tell me the story. A lot of it was science stuff."

"Ed knew a lot?"

"He knew enough to know that it's going to end with a big bang. No other way."

Did she mean Iraq? Iran? North Korea? There were fundamentalists in every religion, extremists who believed only they spoke to the true god. And fundamentalists on the other side responded by nuking them to death. In the meantime millions of children starved in Africa. Wars were declared for oil, no matter the cost in human life. The entire world was falling apart.

Or did Nadine mean the universe would contract and implode back to its origins? The reverse of the Big Bang.

As they talked Nadine zigzagged through the downtown streets. They passed the squat, stony cathedral built long ago by a French archbishop. The church didn't appeal to some. No adobe. No New Mexican mud walls. It was the Santuario at Chimayó that drew la gente. Mud bricks dried in the sun and containing indigenous sun energy. Destined to be washed away by wind and rain, as all things eventually are.

"What the hell are we doing here?" Rosa asked. Nadine had parked in front of the Loretto Chapel.

"A Sun Line runs through here. For Catholics the chapel has a connection to the Virgin Mary. Did you read the story about the angel who brought Joseph and Mary to New Mexico? The angel was helping them escape Herod. Anyway, the angel fell asleep and flew over Egypt. She woke up, looked down, and thought the Rio Grande was the Nile, so she dropped the Holy Family in New Mexico."

Rosa shook her head. "You've been reading too much into *The Da Vinci Code.*"

"No, but Ed did. He read everything. He could read a book faster than I could turn the pages. Sometimes I think he was like a god, or something."

"You loved him?"

"I adored him. He was like a father should be. Pudgy, with thick glasses, like a geek, but kind and gentle. He wouldn't hurt anything. Yeah, he was my protector all right. It ain't fair they murdered him. But I'm going to get those bastards!"

And I'm part of the revenge team, Rosa thought, following a misguided kid. Am I misguided by following her? I don't owe Ed anything. Que descanse en paz. But he had called her, tried to warn her, and he was killed, Bobby said, the way ChupaCabras kill.

Gusts of wind buffeted the car and sent dust and papers scurrying down the deserted and dark streets. A cold low-pressure center was pushing down the east side of the state and funneling the wind through the mountain canyons.

"What now?"

Nadine reached into the glove compartment and took out a flashlight and a map. Rosa caught sight of a small-caliber pistol in the compartment. Nadine was packing.

"Why the pistol?"

"Ed told me to carry it for protection. Don't worry, I'm not going to shoot anybody."

The same warning Bobby had given her. Learn to use a pistol for protection. But it was no longer the drug smugglers who threatened her. If Ed was right, there lay hidden, somewhere on her person or in her things, a bit of DNA from the ChupaCabra she had fought aboard the ship. And those who wanted its DNA had already come after her. The man who broke into her apartment had meant to kill her.

Nadine shone the light on the map and pointed. "The Sun Lines are like arms of the Zia Sun. Ed traced them on the map. Like we were talking about the Golden Carp. That place has a Sun Line running through it. That's why the Golden Carp could live there. That's why the writer could write the story. He grew up there. He knew the place was magical. Ed knew that."

"Ed knew Santa Rosa?"

"He was raised there."

Rosa was surprised. One more revelation about Ed.

"Sun Lines run through all deserts, you know. Like in *Arabian Nights* and where the Bible prophets lived. Even the petroglyphs here were carved by the Indians along Sun Lines. Holy places."

"And here," Rosa said, pointing on the map. "Is Santa Fe on a Sun Line?"

"Nah, not this pendejo place. Too far gone. Too much greed, too much blood. But a Sun Line does run through the chapel."

Rosa looked out the window. The gray Loretto Chapel sat like an old nun praying in the midst of the old city of the holy faith. A city now gone to pot, as Nadine put it. A just-beginning-to-green tree in the courtyard swayed in the wind.

"Climb the thirty-three steps of the winding staircase to the rose window . . ." Nadine intoned.

"What?"

"Ed left the clues we need somewhere in the chapel. We have to find them to know where to go in Roswell." She looked at Rosa. "You know the story. Joseph was a carpenter. He built the staircase."

"Of course I know the story," Rosa retorted.

Everyone in Santa Fe, and many in the rest of the world, knew the story. But one had to have a great deal of faith to believe the legend. A carpenter, some believed it was Joseph the husband of Mary, built the circular staircase in the chapel. Made of wood. Not a nail in it. A miracle. Tourists came from all over the world to view it. Some believed the story, others didn't. All stood in awe of the workmanship.

"But it's closed, it's late."

"I know," Nadine replied. "But Ed taught me how to break into places. Besides, we're only about an hour ahead of Saytir. Come on!"

She opened the door and disappeared into the dark.

"Ah, damn." Rosa groaned and followed.

CHAPTER 9

Twilight had scurried into night.

An eerie silence enveloped the chapel, then a car turned into the Inn at Loretto's parking lot, its lights momentarily stabbing the darkness. A door banged, a valet called, then the light and the sounds were gone.

On the street a couple, probably guests at the inn, passed by, bending into the wind. Rosa stiffened, but the two went by without noticing them. A car rumbled down the narrow street in front of the chapel, then all was quiet.

Rosa sniffed the air. What did Nadine say: we're only an hour ahead of Saytir? Surely the beast could not enter the chapel.

"Don't bet on it," Nadine said, studiously picking at the door lock.

"This is against the law," Rosa whispered, picturing herself in the Santa Fe jail, calling her parents and trying to explain how she had gotten there.

"Not really," Nadine replied. "Churches are sanctus, sanctus—you know."

"Sanctuaries."

"Whatever. Wasn't the whole state a sanctuary once? Ed told me. People worry too much about borders. If there were no borders there would be no worry. People are afraid of other people. Beats me. They're all the same inside."

Rosa wasn't in the right frame of mind to discuss the current jingoistic feelings surfacing in the country. Demagogues were making their reputations by stirring up anti-Mexican propaganda. What bothered her right then was that they might be spotted.

"Is there any other way to get in? Why not ask at the hotel's reception desk?"

"No way they would let us in. Plus, we don't want to involve others. Too dangerous."

"You got me involved."

"No, you got yourself involved. You have what they want. They will kill you for it. You have to get Saytir before he gets you. It's that simple. Besides, you're numero uno ChupaCabra woman. La mera, mera pistolera."

She laughed softly and pushed the door open. A warm, sanctified air composed of candle wax and some kind of spirituality greeted them.

They entered the alcove between the chapel entrance and the gift shop. The place was dark. Empty.

"The staircase," Nadine whispered. She turned on the flashlight and Rosa followed her into the chapel.

Even in the dim light the circular staircase was a thing of beauty. The work of an artisan whose skills might have been honed in an Italian workshop where the likes of a Michelangelo once studied. Or a shop in Nazareth where Joseph planed fragrant cedar planks while patiently mulling over the inspired pregnancy of his wife.

Or, Rosa thought as the light played on the shining wood, it's the good honest work of a New Mexican carpenter. She knew the craftsmen of the state had evolved from humble, colonial beginnings to the genius of a Patrocino Barela. Yes, he, or someone like him, could have built the magical staircase.

"We need to find the *immaculate pillar.*"

"The immaculate pillar?" Rosa repeated. "I don't get it."

"I don't know this place," Nadine replied. "Ed said you do."

"Yes, but I don't know about an immaculate pillar."

"Now you tell me. Okay. Ed said to shine the light from up there. The rose window upstairs is directly in the Sun Line." She aimed the flashlight at the choir loft. "You need to climb up there."

"Me?"

"Who else?"

Reluctantly, Rosa took the flashlight. I've come this far, she thought as she made her way up the staircase. Beneath her the wood creaked and groaned.

The Sisters of Loretto and their students had used the staircase for many years. Many a high mass had been sung from the choir loft. But Rosa felt she was violating a trust because the staircase had been closed to use years ago. Now it was only a tourist attraction. The staircase made two 360-degree turns from the floor to the choir loft, reminding Rosa of pictures she had seen of the DNA double helix. Two strands of chromosomes containing the genes of humanity. Did the carpenter who built the staircase have a vision? Did he get his plan from a dream in which he peered into the spiraling DNA helix? Was he God-inspired?

The chapel was part of Rosa's heritage. Climbing toward the rose window, she did not think of heaven, but of a past time, the time of her beginnings in that string of DNA and the genes that dictated so much of who she was.

I am, she thought, more than the conglomeration of genes. Nadine's story that Saytir was looking for her because she had in her possession some bit of ChupaCabra DNA had Rosa thinking of genes.

She stepped onto the choir loft and aimed the light on the small but exquisite rose window. Such stained-glass windows were a legacy of the Gothic cathedral era. Like any circular mandala, the radiance of light that flowed through the window embodied the human aspiration for completeness and balance. Harmony. Wholeness. Here at the chapel it was the radiance of divine spirit that poured through when the sun shone on the glass.

Not the west rose window of Notre Dame in Paris, thought Rosa, but lovely anyway. She turned and looked down at Nadine.

"What now?"

"Shine the light around everywhere—on the stations of the cross on the walls, on the altar, everywhere. We need to find the immaculate pillar."

Rosa shone the light on the walls. What did immaculate pillar mean? The pillar of light reported by those who had experienced an out-of-body experience? Those caught in the zone between life and death often reported they had seen a pillar of light as their spirit left their body. Was the staircase the immaculate pillar? Like Joseph's ladder?

She turned the light on the altar and moved it slowly back and forth, experiencing anew the beauty. She had been to mass and weddings in the chapel, but this was a unique experience. Surreal. She had broken into the chapel with this girl who promised to save her life, and here she was shining a light on the crucifix. Two angels stood on either side. The Sacred Heart of Jesus hung on the north wall.

Then it hit her. There it was! A small pillar holding a candle in front of the statue of the Virgin Mary.

"Nadine," she whispered, but Nadine had already seen it and was leaping over the railing.

Immaculate pillar, Rosa thought. I should have known it was related to the Immaculate Conception. But she had thought the pillar would be large; this was only a four-foot candlestand. She hurried down to Nadine, who had already moved the stand to expose a CD wrapped in a plastic baggie.

"Holy moly! This is it! Hello Roswell. Good-bye Saytir."

"What's in it?"

"Directions," Nadine replied. "First we have to take care of Ed."

"What do you mean?"

"Find him!"

Rosa frowned. "He's dead."

"Yeah, but we have to claim his body. Ed was a martyr. He will be the one who rescues Roswell from the C-Force project!"

Rosa didn't have time to respond. Someone had entered the chapel. Rosa's survival instinct kicked into gear. A ChupaCabra!

She pointed the light and illuminated a pair of red, reptilian eyes.

"Saytir!" Nadine cried and froze. Saytir had come for the CD they had found.

Rosa stared at the form that seemed to shift from the hulk of a big man to the monster she remembered from the ship. A ChupaCabra! Saytir was a shape-shifter! He could move from one body form into another!

She paused. Or was the shape in front of her an illusion? Maybe cloning technology wasn't just a biological shift! Maybe it involved electromagnetic forces wired into the nervous system. Saytir could change his body form by using thought control! Virtual reality was real. Electrical impulses allowed him to change his form at will! And maybe what she was looking at was not form at all, but an image!

No need to take chances, Rosa thought. Whatever was there *was there*!

She threw the flashlight as hard as she could, striking Saytir between the eyes. The form melted away.

"Come on!" Rosa cried, grabbing Nadine's cold hand.

They ran out of the chapel past the gift shop and into the street. They didn't stop running until they reached the car.

CHAPTER 10

 "I panicked," Nadine said. "It felt good."

"Good?" Rosa asked, puzzled.

"Yeah, look. I'm out of breath. I'm trembling. Damn, sister, this feels good!"

"Just the adrenaline," Rosa said, then asked, "Was that Saytir?"

"Yes. Or maybe one of his forms. He can take different forms. If he's wired, he can be just about anything."

"Wired?"

"Saytir's more than a himit. The lab went a step further. He can morph because himit's wired."

"Morph into different forms?" Rosa mused. "Just like the devil." The devil appeared in many guises to do its mischief. Was Saytir a devil, one of the many who tumbled into the world when Lucifer fell?

Nadine shook her head. "Ed didn't believe in the devil. All these things they're doing with DNA, cloning the space aliens and ChupaCabras, humans are doing it."

Rosa nodded in agreement.

"Ed said it's humans who can be crazy as hell. I think he meant humans are capable of anything. Look at the war that's going on right now. Why can't humans save the children who are suffering instead of playing god with cloning?"

"Not all of us are playing god—hey, where to?"

"Roswell. The CD has Ed's instructions. Vamos."

They headed out of town on Old Santa Fe Trail and took U.S. 285 to Clines Corners.

"How well did you know Ed?" Rosa asked as Santa Fe disappeared behind them.

She herself was beginning to remember more about Ed. Bits and pieces of his character were returning.

For one thing, Ed had labeled every part of the carcass of the dead cat in the biology experiment. And, as was found out later, he had not killed the cat; it was a dead cat stored in the biology lab. She remembered the silence in the room as the science teacher looked at the cat. After he calmed down he walked around the desk.

"Damn. He got every part right," the teacher muttered. He had looked up at the silent, expectant students. "Every damn part."

"He was my savior," Nadine replied. "He knew I wasn't like the others. He took a chance. What everyone needs, no matter who you are, is someone to care. You know what I mean? Ed was like that. A genius, a nerd, a loving nerd, open, always helping others. That was his creed: help others. He loved the world, he really did. He was always saying, it's up to us to stand up against evil. I learned a lot from him. And it was easy. Like our minds just talked to each other without words."

Rosa nodded. Like love. That's what she felt for Bobby. And for teaching. As a young assistant professor she had been eager to teach, and that meant inspiring her students with the same love of literature that moved her intellect and emotions. She could talk an entire period on any of the novels she taught. But the real joy came when suddenly a light would go on in one of the blank faces. One of them would have an epiphany into the real depth and nature of the story being read, and a face would light up with joy.

"Joy."

"Yeah, that's the way it was," Nadine agreed. "Thanks for saving me back there."

"I guess I'm into this as deep as a charge of breaking and entering," Rosa responded.

Nadine smiled. "Deeper."

"Get them before they get you?"

"Exactly."

"But they could have found this bit of ChupaCabra DNA they're looking for in my apartment. On my clothes or the bag I carried aboard ship, or the camera—" She thought of the photo José had taken of the ChupaCabra.

"Know what I think?" Nadine asked. "I think you absorbed the DNA into your body. Into your hair. They need to destroy you to get to it."

Rosa shivered. It was crazy. She couldn't absorb DNA. And if she had, what did it mean? Had she at any point touched the blood or saliva of the ChupaCabra? She *had* touched the blood on Chuco's head the night she found him dead. His skull had been punctured by the teeth of the ChupaCabra. Saliva. She looked down at her hands and felt queasy.

"Ed said there's a Grendel in all of us. You remember the story of Beowulf and Grendel. Grendel is the monster in the forest. Beowulf has to kill Grendel because the monster eats up the people. Especially virgins. Those monsters are always eating virgins. Even King Kong. A Grendel in us, and we project him, like a movie, not on a screen but into real life. The monster becomes real, so we have to destroy Grendel."

She glanced at Rosa and smiled an *ain't I smart* smile.

Yes, Rosa thought. Researching the monsters of ancient legends and myths led me to ChupaCabra. The story started somewhere in

Puerto Rico, somewhere where the C-Force biologists first created Saytir and his bunch of himits. But the truth was that ChupaCabras, and all the monsters in the folktales of the world, were part of human history.

"The ghosts and monsters of our past live in our memory," Rosa said. "They live in our collective memory. In our blood. For millions of years we have been projecting those monsters into reality. They become real. Or we think they're real."

"This time they are real," Nadine said.

Rosa knew the monsters in the subconscious were only images, but she had seen a real ChupaCabra aboard ship. She had read about the gods, beasts, and monsters in many mythologies. She understood how different cultures used such beings in their stories. She thought she had a good grasp on the function of storytelling, but the ChupaCabra she had met was real.

Did believing intensely in the monster make it real? Or does one slip into a neurotic state when one begins to believe the monster is real?

"You believe the clones are real?" Rosa whispered.

"Better believe it. And C-Force wants to use them to rule the world. Use the aliens and ChupaCabras as destroyers. That's what Ed found out."

"Did he say to get rid of the monsters?"

"That's the mission," Nadine replied.

"Destroy them?"

"Yes. They're being created by evil men. They will be used to cause violence, wars, murder, rape, abuse—all the bad things. For C-Force the monsters are an army."

"What of the monsters inside us?" Rosa asked. "To destroy them, do we destroy ourselves?"

In the dark Nadine nodded.

"There are other ways," Rosa continued. "Psychologists can help one get in touch with the demons in the mind. We know more about the unconscious. We don't have to destroy the person to get rid of the Grendels. With psychiatric help we bring them to the surface, deal with them, and learn how to get rid of them. Or at least control them. Priests can help, also rabbis, counselors, the medications of doctors, curanderas, and healers who understand the psyche."

And still dark voices from the past lingered and returned to haunt anew each generation. The DNA memory stretched back to the earliest days of humans on earth when the jungles and dark forests were full of Grendels, full of ChupaCabras.

"Like that movie where the priest exorcises the devil? I saw it. But the priest could never completely get rid of the devil. It's too late for that, sister. Besides, this is not a movie. This is for real. And remember, these are not devils like the guy that gave Eve the apple. These are monsters being created by humans."

Maybe she's right, Rosa thought. Maybe we can never completely get rid of the ghosts that haunt us. The streets were full of people haunted by their individual demons. But witch hunting was not the answer. Enough was known about of the workings of the mind to expel the ghosts. Else, why had psychiatry spent hundreds of years trying to solve the riddles?

"There are no easy answers," she acknowledged, knowing that the dark voices in the soul still led the sick to their deaths.

Outside the wind was a lonely, raging creature blowing over the empty plain. Gusts buffeted the car. The anguished cry of la Llorona filled the night. La Llorona had killed her children. She searched for them on the road to Roswell. The simple stories of the past created fear in children, made them go to bed shivering. Made some wet their mattresses.

But the story of the wailing woman seemed tame compared to the monsters Nadine described. La Llorona put a little fear into children, made them behave and get home early. The story kept the children out of harm's way. The C-Force project had to do with the end of the world. Cloning in the new century created dread. Angst, philosophers would say. A dread so deep it was affecting human nature, bringing on the fall of the civilized world.

"Damn, I hate to be so pessimistic."

"I know," Nadine replied. "And so we have to create a fire to save the world."

CHAPTER 11

They stopped at Clines Corners, a place midway between Alburquerque and Santa Rosa, a town Rosa knew. The high plateau country around Clines Corners was pleasing and open. Rosa alighted from the car and looked into the darkness. The land here was much like the Hi-Lo country Max Evans described in his books. Cattle country. Mule deer ran in the mesas, and antelope grazed where the land flattened out. Here, winter blizzards could be vicious, but the summers were cool and pleasant; the wind a constant as it swept across the mesas and canyons. But tonight there was an ominous feeling in the spring wind that sent occasional tumbleweeds rolling across the interstate. Rosa drew her jacket tight.

"Need gas," Nadine said.

One of two truckers passing gave her a head's up. "Hey, honey, you got two low rear tires. Heavy load?"

"A dead body," Nadine replied.

"Yeah, a dead body. Hey, me and my buddy are going to party in Tucumcari. Why don't you two chickadees join us."

Nadine blew him off. "Nobody parties in Tucumcari. Besides, you're old enough to be my grandpa."

The two truckers laughed, patted each other on the back, and headed for their rig, out of the gusting wind and toward their rendezvous.

Nadine shook her head. "Guys like that should stop in Santa Rosa and pay their respects to the Golden Carp. Partying in Tucumcari is like an ox-moron."

"Oxymoron."

"Go inside. I'll be a while."

Rosa headed into the restaurant. The brightly lit place was empty. She went to the bathroom and returned to buy coffee and a cream pie. Nadine sat at a table, her laptop plugged in, reading the CD they found in the chapel.

Rosa shrugged, drank her coffee, and munched on the cream pie.

They hadn't been there five minutes when two men entered and sat at a corner table. Dressed in dark suits and wearing black topcoats, they looked out of place. Men in black, caricatures of FBI agents, or mafia. Not the usual tourist or local cowboy.

Rosa saw Nadine frown. She unplugged her computer and hurried to Rosa.

"Clones," she whispered. "Let's go." She glanced toward the sleepy clerk at the counter and slipped a package of gum into her pocket.

Rosa followed Nadine to the car. Of all the stories told about Clines Corners—deaths and adventures, desperados and state cop shootouts, drug busts—none had ever been told about clones.

Rosa glanced back over her shoulder. The two men hadn't followed.

"How do you know they're clones?"

Nadine didn't answer. Without turning on the headlights she gunned the car toward Alburquerque. Miles down the road she suddenly swerved, cut across the median and turned east, barely escaping getting hit by an eighteen wheeler that barreled past them.

"Damn!" Rosa exclaimed.

Nadine straightened out the car and headed back to Clines Corners and the Roswell exit.

"Trying to lose them," Nadine responded. "Esos muertos use those global positioning satellites. Coordinated by C-Force in Roswell."

"The lab in Roswell?"

"Yes."

"Why call them muertos?"

"They're dead. Zombies."

"Did the CD provide any information?"

"Yes. Ed knew how to get it to me without getting me killed. And if I didn't make it, the CD was going to you. That's why it was at the chapel. But I'm here, we're here. God, I'm so glad you're helping me."

"How am I helping?"

"You're going to be witness and write the story. Hey, you're a professor. People listen to professors. We need you to expose C-Force."

"This feels like a science fiction movie," Rosa said.

"Yeah, but this is real," Nadine answered. "Really real."

"How did you know those two back there were clones?"

"I see it in their eyes. And they create static. You know, I can hear them."

"They didn't say anything," Rosa said.

"You have to listen closely. The worst part is they know we're here. Be alert."

"How can I tell?"

Nadine shrugged. "They only have three fingers on each hand. See?" She made a claw.

"Don't kid me."

Nadine laughed. "Okay, okay. But you can hear them. You know, telepathically."

"But they, and the ones in Santa Fe, look human."

"Human skin. C-Force developed some silicone human skin. Shape-shifters. You saw Saytir. He moves in and out of his skin."

Rosa nodded. "Hard to believe. Reproducing alien clones?"

"By the hundred thousands."

"Ed found out?"

"Yup."

The star people, Rosa thought. Uncle Billy said they have always been here. Are we descendents of the star people? Did some gigantic meteor crash to earth, bringing stardust that fell into ancient, murky seas and evolve? Into us? Meteors crashing into the earth was common knowledge. The evidence was there. But this was different. What if long ago a spaceship had hurled itself across the galactic night to slam into the Earth.

Or what if it did not crash. What if the so-called incidents of crashing meteorites were really UFOs? They had burrowed into the earth, or the sea. For centuries they had lain dormant, now the descendents were coming out to look around.

They were here. Or, they *are* here.

"But these aren't the UFO aliens?"

"Of course not. The UFO brethren are nice. Talk to Marcy, she knows all about them. The clones are being created by C-Force."

"C-Force must possess extraordinary abilities," Rosa said. "If they can clone ChupaCabras, you get a super monster—" She shook her head. "I'm beginning to think weird."

"Right on, sister," Nadine replied, and gave her a high five. "Weird is good. Think of all the weird kids in the world that need help. Just like me. Ed helped me. Weird is good, but those scientists in Roswell are not good."

They had passed no cars on the dark road, but suddenly a flashing red light appeared out of nowhere, bathing the interior of the car with its bloodlike color. A high, shrieking cry filled the night.

Nadine cursed.

The light bore down on them, like the red, burning eyes of a ChupaCabra, forcing Nadine to slow down and finally park on the shoulder of the road.

She cursed again, reached into the glove compartment, and pulled out the pistol.

"This is not good," she whispered as she tucked the pistol into her vest.

"You don't need that," Rosa protested. "It's a police car."

"Shhhh," Nadine replied. "Let me handle this."

They waited. The red, swirling light cast devilish shadows across their faces. Finally a cop knocked on the window.

Nadine rolled down the window. "Officer, sorry, sorry, I know I was speeding, but my friend is very sick. I have to get her to a doctor."

The cop shone a light on Rosa. "Very sick, huh? Step outside."

"Is this necessary? Really, give me a ticket. I have to get her—"

"Step outside!" the policeman ordered.

Nadine stepped out.

"What's in your trunk?"

"Just clothes. My friend's—"

"Open it."

"Please. I have to get her to a doctor—"

"Open it!"

Rosa watched as Nadine and the officer walked around the back. The trunk's door flipped up, and an instant later a shot startled Rosa. She jumped out and rushed to the back of the car.

The policeman lay on the ground. Nadine stood over him with the pistol in her hand.

"Oh God. You killed him!"

"He's a himit," Nadine said. "I had to. He saw what I'm carrying."

Rosa looked into the trunk. It was filled with packages marked "plastic explosives."

"Explosives?" Rosa questioned. "Why?"

"For Ed," Nadine replied. "Look."

She picked up the cop's flashlight and shone it on the himit's dead body. The human face was slowly disintegrating. In its place something like the hideous face of a ChupaCabra appeared.

Rosa turned away and vomited bitter coffee and cream pie.

CHAPTER 12

Nadine took the himit's phone and stuffed it into a vest pocket. Then she leaned down and grabbed his feet.

"Help me push himit off the road."

Rosa hesitated. She remembered the ChupaCabra aboard the cruise ship. It had rushed at her, but it had not touched her. Now she had to help dispose of a strange alien or clone or whatever it was that Nadine called himits. The thing kept disintegrating before her eyes.

"Come on, himit's dead."

"Why?" she muttered.

"Saytir will find himit. This buys time. Come on!"

Grimacing, Rosa grabbed a foot and helped Nadine pull the clone to the road's shoulder. They pushed and the body rolled down the incline, leaving a squishy sound in its wake.

Nadine got in the clone's car, started it, aimed it off the side of the road and jumped out. The car rolled slowly over the edge and into the gully.

She ran back to Rosa. "You okay?" she asked.

Rosa nodded. But she wasn't okay. Nadine had just shot and killed a strange creature that changed form before their eyes. Whatever they were, they were real, but what did *real* mean?

"Let's go!" Nadine cried, slamming the trunk lid shut. They jumped in the car and she burned rubber roaring away from the scene.

Miles down the road she tossed the clone's phone out the window. "No telling if himit phoned in our position, but they know we're headed for Roswell."

"Why did you have to kill him?"

"Himit."

"Okay, himit. Why?"

"He would have killed us. He saw the explosives."

"What are they for?"

"I told you. They're for Ed's plan."

"But Ed's dead."

"So it's up to us," Nadine replied.

"Why not call the police, tell them what you know?"

"Are you kidding? We can't trust anyone. Not in Roswell. They killed Ed. Don't forget that. C-Force has enough money to buy the entire town. Saytir's got the himits looking for us, and you saw the cop back there. Wasn't a cop. The only one we can trust in Roswell is Marcy, the librarian. By now she should have downloaded everything into her computer. She is so good at that technical stuff. If we get separated, go to her, but not the cops. They've probably covered up Ed's death by now. Called his death an accident."

Rosa nodded. That's what Bobby intimated. Someone in the Roswell police was not forthcoming with information.

"So there are clones in the police force?"

"Some. They have infiltrated a lot of places—and not just in Roswell. Saytir has a lot of power. He spreads money around. Has bought more souls than the devil."

"He sounds like the devil," Rosa mused. "Have we created a devil?"

"Not us, they," Nadine corrected. "The scientists and biologists who work for C-Force. Greedy traitors. They're not interested in science; they got into it for the money. But now they live in fear. They can't control Saytir."

"What is he?"

"Himit," Nadine corrected her. "Saytir's one of the originals. The DNA they used created a super himit, and now himit controls C-Force. He got like really powerful. Ed said even the government men, and the military, all those involved in the project, are afraid of Saytir."

"What is the C-Force project?"

"Something about genomes. I don't know the technical stuff."

"Aren't you afraid?"

"Ed didn't teach me the emotion of fear. Human emotions are fine, but fear is bad. Fear makes you freeze up. I'll go one-on-one with Saytir."

Nadine *was* tough, thought Rosa. Go one-on-one with a monster? And she meant it. Why? For Ed. She was willing to do anything to avenge Ed.

They drove in silence for a while. In her mind Rosa was piecing together the details she knew, trying to make a coherent picture of the puzzle bits. At every turn a new piece was added, and it was totaling up. But still, there were missing pieces. And what could she and Nadine do against a conspiracy so big and powerful that it had gotten out of the government's control?

And who was to know which government agencies were involved? CIA? FBI? The White House? Secret military units? After all, it was the military that clamped down on information after the famous 1947 UFO crash. Had C-Force been operating all along? Part of Project Blue Book? Part of the team that investigated the 1964 Lonnie Zamora report of the UFO that he claimed landed near Socorro? Was C-Force just a new name for a series of names the government had used to cover up its role in the matter?

Rosa knew bits and pieces of events, names, and places that had become part of New Mexico UFO folklore, but she had never dug deep into the phenomena. She had scanned reports on the Internet. UFO sightings were worldwide. But what Nadine had described and what Rosa had just seen were bigger than any account of a UFO sighting.

And what could the two of them do against Saytir? The ChupaCabra she met on the cruise ship had been monstrous, a beast controlled by the drug traffickers. The drug smugglers made billions by controlling evil forces. Now C-Force had Saytir, who was a hundred times more deadly than the ChupaCabra because Saytir embodied both a ChupaCabra and a foreign life-form.

How strange, she thought. Innocent visitors from outer space had come to earth, crashed their spaceships into the New Mexico desert, and left traces of their DNA on the sand. Now evil men were using that DNA to create an army of clones. Unstoppable clones.

And the explosives. Did Nadine hope to stop the project using the explosives?

"What about the explosives?"

"Plastic. Ed got only the best. Powerful stuff. I could blow up half of Roswell."

"Is that your plan?"

"Of course not. We don't hurt the innocent. Ed will tell us what to do."

"Where? When?"

"First stop, the UFO museum in Roswell."

"Why only bits of information at a time?"

"Ed knew they were after him. If he described the mission in one package and Saytir discovered the plan, then that would be the end. That's what himit was after back at the chapel. So Ed hid the instructions in different places. As a safeguard."

"Him. Not her. Do they have gender?"

"Gender?"

"Like male and female. Can they reproduce?"

"No. Clones are sterile."

"Did C-Force ever clone a female?"

"Yeah, they did!" Nadine exclaimed. "They cloned a *she-it*." She burst out laughing. "You get it? A sheit!"

Rosa waited then asked, "What happened?"

"They only had enough of the X chromosome to make one."

"What happened to her, I mean, the sheit?"

"Just like a female, she was too independent. She got loose. Ed said this whole thing is like the Garden of Eden story. C-Force is acting like God, taking DNA from the space aliens and the ChupaCabra and creating monsters. And guess what? They couldn't control the sheit. Ed used to laugh. 'That sheit is like Eve in the garden,' he said."

"You mean when Eve ate the apple?"

"Toe jam!" Nadine laughed. "She busted loose! They couldn't control Eve! Ed called her Eve. You know the story. Eve was told not to eat the apple because she would know what she could really do on her own. But she did it! Just like us! Roswell, here we come!"

She stepped on the gas pedal and the heavily loaded car shuddered and shook as the gauge clocked near a hundred miles per hour. They zoomed down the road, bucking the night wind that raged across the Roswell desert.

CHAPTER 13

Nadine said, "I know, I know, this is getting weirder and weirder." She laughed, dissipating some of the tension. "Like that girl in the *Wizard of Oz*. Dorothy through a looking glass. Remember?"

She opened a gum package, popped a piece in her mouth, and passed the package to Rosa.

"Thanks. You've read a lot?" Rosa asked.

"No, not at all. Ed used to read to me. He loved to read. We would go to the library and he and Marcy would talk for hours. And we would take books home. Dozens. It's funny, but I memorized every book he read to me."

"What do you mean, memorized?"

"You know, like the entire book would go into my mind. I know every word. Like one day he read *War and Peace*. That's a friggin' big book, you know. You could use that sucker for a pillow. Anyway, it's like I have the entire book in me."

"Can you quote from it?"

"No. I'm not that good. The book is in me—I know all the characters, the scenes that took place. It's like I know every single sentence."

"But you can't use it?"

"Use? I never thought literature was to *use*. Ed said the books would make me a better person. You know, educated. He read me *The Odyssey, The Iliad, Don Quixote,* travel books, legends like Beowulf and Grendel, all the Aztec myths. He knew the Mayan calendar inside out. He even read the Harry Potter books. Just last week we were reading murder mysteries by Chicanas. I really got into them. Those Chicanas are real, you know. Kick-ass real. And he read me a lot of New Mexico writers. He loved them. He said they're every bit as good as those so-called big-time writers who make a lot of money."

Rosa had to smile. Very few writers in the state made much money.

"Some of the books were audiotapes I listened to at night. And symphonies, mariachi, rancheras, you name it. Fifties rock and roll. He loved the fifties. Say it was Beethoven night. He would place the CD player by my bed. I put on earphones and in the morning entire symphonies were in me. I could feel them. That's absolutely the best way to learn. Once Ed checked out *The Divine Comedy* CD. I knew every corner of hell by just hearing it while I slept. You know, they say if you play music or read books to a baby in the womb, the baby hears/feels it. That's how I learned."

"The fetus in its sack of water . . . water is a good conductor of sound," Rosa noted. "Whales and dolphins communicate through water."

"And space, sister. All that stuff coming from out there."

"Out there?"

"Ed said they're out there. Angels, he and Marcy called them. Maybe like angels. A kind of life we don't know. They're not those little green men, or those weird machines they show in the space/fantasy movies."

"Did he say what they look like?"

"Maybe human. He and Marcy were into this parallel universe

thing. Space/Humans are running around this world, right next to us, but we can't see them. They live in their own time/space universe. They're so advanced in time that they can make flying saucers, you know, spaceships. Most humans can't see that kind of life around them."

A metaphor? thought Rosa. The idea of parallel universes had been advanced by those physicists who studied the time/space phenomena. Time/space was a flow of some kind of ether, a river, or many rivers, flowing through the cosmos. Each river was occupied by a particular kind of life. Life-forms or images. Some born early during the Big Bang were very advanced. Far beyond human conception. Such a theory would explain a lot of things.

"That would explain a lot of things," Rosa mused. "Anyway, when Ed read to you, or you listened to a CD, did you hear only words?"

"Words, words, words. Oh no. I could hear the ideas. The ideas were in the air and they were passing through my skin into my brain." Nadine laughed. "Whatever little brain I have."

They talked, tossing Ed's ideas back and forth as they neared Roswell. Suddenly Nadine pulled to the side of the road and parked. She pointed at a series of lights flying over the city, a formation of seven.

"See that?"

Rosa looked.

"UFOs. They're here. What the hell do people expect? They built a UFO museum and E.T. came to visit. You know, like kids go on field trips." In the dark she smiled her enigmatic smile.

"Those aren't UFOs," Rosa said, peering into the dark, blustery sky. "They look like airplanes. Maybe helicopters."

"Every monkey to his swing, Ed used to say. But helicopters don't move like that. Keep watching."

Rosa watched as the slow-moving lights made a wide turn and appeared directly over them. The lights grew brighter, kaleidoscopic.

A thing of mystery and beauty. A gentle kinetic energy, like music, flowed through her. She felt her pulse racing. Whatever was flying over them was something magical.

Suddenly the lights whooshed away. They were gone in an instant.

"Ever see a helicopter do that?"

Rosa shook her head. But surely there were other explanations. Weather balloons, a rocket from the Spaceport America near Alamogordo, experimental sky planes. There were air force bases nearby. But seven? In formation then zooming away. What could do that?

"They're out there," Nadine continued, "and they're not too happy with what C-Force is doing with the DNA of the first colonizers."

"Colonizers?"

"Ed said the angels from space are colonists. You know, they live here. Just like NASA now wants to colonize the moon and Mars. But the air force shot one of their ships down in 1947. They had these missiles at White Sands, and they shot it down."

"But the few accounts I've read of the '47 crash say it was a weather balloon," Rosa insisted. "What really fell near Corona was a weather balloon."

She was still doubting, even though the energy from the spaceships had filled her with a sense of awe. What if they were real? The rational part of her mind didn't want to accept that.

"That's what they want you to believe," Nadine said as she started the car and drove on. "But you saw Saytir. You saw the himit I shot. Get over it, sister. No time left to doubt. It's up to us to stop it."

"What next?" Rosa asked.

"The UFO museum. The last clue is in the museum."

They drove down sleepy Main Street Roswell, the UFO capital of the world. The chamber of commerce boosters had created the UFO museum and a yearly summer festival that drew thousands of visitors. Before 1947 nobody in his right mind visited Roswell. Some parents sent their kids to the military academy, and the school had produced some well-known graduates, but other than that there were not too many reasons to visit Roswell.

But the UFO museum had established Roswell as the UFO capital, and the town's economy profited.

Nadine parked the car down the street from the museum.

"We have to take a chance," she whispered. "Use the alley." She motioned and Rosa followed her into the alley behind the museum.

Another break-in, Rosa thought. What would I say: I do research on aliens from outer space and I didn't want to bother anyone so I just broke in.

Nadine tried the door. It swung open, but no alarm sounded. The flashlight revealed a frown on her face.

"Not good," she whispered.

They entered a storage room full of crates and boxes. Nadine led into the main area of exhibits. The glass cases contained the memorabilia of UFO history, Roswell style. One held the body of what an alien was supposed to look like. Others held purported pieces of UFOs. There were photos of the ranch where the UFO landed, military personnel, an old weathered rancher—photos taken over the years of hovering UFOs all over the world.

In the middle of the room stood the most recent glass case. They could tell it was freshly installed. Nadine shone the light to reveal the body of a man. He stared at them, a look of disbelief on his face.

A sign hung around his neck read: "This man did not believe the aliens visited Roswell. Therefore we call him 'THE DOUBTER.'"

"Ed!" Nadine cried. "Oh my God, it's Ed!"

She fell to her knees, sobbing.

CHAPTER 14

Nadine dropped the flashlight and rocked back and forth, crying, "Oh damn, look what they did to him! They crucified him. They murdered him . . . they want people to laugh at him . . . what did they do? Cover him in wax? I'm going to get them! I'm going to get them!"

Rosa picked up the flashlight and shone the light on the body. There was Ed. Same build, and something in the face was familiar. Cruel death had not taken away his nobility. His look was one of defiance.

Did they mean to exhibit him forever?

Thoughts ran through her mind as she stared at the body. The Egyptians, in ancient times, had used all sorts of oils to protect the body encased in a winding-sheet. Placed in a sarcophagus in a tomb under the dry desert, in the Valley of the Kings, the mummy would last forever. The soul of the dead person had a body to return to from time to time. They molded face masks of gold for the really important pharaohs. The Tutankhamen mask had been found. It was worth millions.

Would Ed last forever? Was this Saytir's revenge? A warning to the world not to oppose C-Force?

Had they performed an autopsy? Saved Ed's organs in Canopic jars like the Egyptians? Had they dipped the body in a vat of wax? Despite the hurried job there remained something noble in his features.

Courage. Yes, the courage of a revolutionary. The eyes stared back like in photos she had seen of Emiliano Zapata. Where is Zapata when we need him? she thought. Or Pancho Villa?

Ed was a revolutionary, not for land for the Mexican farmers, but to save the world from C-Force. Ed had died a cruel death. Was he now crying out for revenge?

"Yes," Nadine moaned, "I will avenge his death."

Rosa thought back to the Ed she had known in high school. She remembered that one day he had offered her an apple at lunch-time. He smiled. He had an angelic smile. His nose was always in a book. His science project could have gone to state, but he didn't enter. Later she learned that he volunteered at the food bank, delivering food to the elderly.

And a while back one of her classmates had called. She mentioned that Ed had been fired for leading a protest against the war in Iraq. Many memories flashed through her mind as she stared at the petrified mummy that was now Ed.

Nadine whispered, "See what they did to him? Kids will come and point and say he didn't believe. He was so good, and look at him now. A warning from Saytir."

"But the police? Surely they can—"

"Saytir is the police. C-Force is a big conspiracy. It began in 1947 when they covered up the UFO crash. They shot it down so they had to hide the facts. They can cover up anything."

Rosa reached down and pulled Nadine to her feet. She looked into her dark, fathomless eyes. Nadine had been crying, but there were no tears. Her eyes were dry as the desert around Roswell.

"I'm sorry, Nadine."

Nadine nodded. "I'll get them," she whispered. Grabbing the flashlight she smashed the glass. She reached in and yanked the sign around Ed's neck.

"He wasn't a doubter!" she shouted. "He was the Believer!"

Her cry echoed in the room; then from the silence came a faint reply.

"Yes, he was."

They turned to see the red, glowing eyes of Saytir at the far end of the room. The same flaming eyes Rosa knew belonged to ChupaCabras.

"Saytir!"

"Nadine," he replied, devilish laughter gurgling from deep in his sulfurous lungs. "You have something I want."

He moved forward and in the dim light his form changed into a form Rosa knew well: the ChupaCabra! He raised his arms, exposing sharp claws, glistening nails, a leathery cloak that rustled like the thin, silky stuff of bat wings. The eyes burned like live coals. The rotten smell of an ancient, stagnant swamp filled the room.

"Give it up," he challenged, his screech like that of a vampire when it attacks.

"What do you want?" Nadine cried.

"You," Saytir answered. "Come home!"

"No . . ." Nadine went limp.

Rosa startled. He had a strange power over Nadine! But Rosa had no time to analyze. She reacted instinctively and quickly, pushing a display case in front of the advancing beast. The glass exploded in shards that temporarily blinded Saytir. He was fearful of seeing his reflection in the pieces of glass.

Those few seconds were enough for Rosa to grab Nadine's arm and run. They sprinted out of the room, crashing against display cases as they raced to the back room.

They dashed in, bolted the door, and stood pressed against it.

Both knew Saytir could destroy the door, but the only response was silence.

"He's gone?" Rosa panted.

"No," Nadine replied, gritting her teeth. "He's waiting for me—"

"I thought it was me, the DNA I'm supposed to carry."

Nadine shook her head. "He wants to know where Ed hid the instructions."

"That reveal the C-Force lab," Rosa said.

"Yes. Or the names of anyone who helped Ed. Saytir knows I won't talk . . . and—" She looked at Rosa. "And you don't know. I have to get you out of here," Nadine whispered. She looked plaintively at Rosa for an instant, then jumped into action. "Come on! We don't have much time!"

She opened the door that led into the alley and peered out. In the dim light dozens of large-eyed UFO aliens rushed past her. Nadine jumped back as one of the aliens smacked her in the face.

"Damn you!" she cried and pushed away the green, rubbery alien.

Someone had ordered boxes of the alien costumes, and the wind had broken the boxes apart. Puffed up by the strong gusts, the costumes floated eerily down the alley, making it seem as if a band of space aliens had landed in the dark of night to attack Roswell.

"You okay?" asked Rosa.

Nadine nodded. "Looks clear."

"But Saytir is still—"

"I think what we saw was an image, a projection of Saytir. Ed said they know how to transfer their images through lasers. Make them real. Take the car and meet me at the library. Remember, we need to guard the car. We need the explosives."

She handed Rosa the car keys.

"And you?"

"I'm going back—"

Rosa grabbed her arm. "Go back in there? You're crazy!"

"I have to free Ed."

"What if Saytir's waiting?"

"I know what he wants. Get the CD in my laptop to Marcy. She knows what to do."

"I can't leave you alone—"

"Trust me. If we split up, one of us will make it."

She handed Rosa the flashlight, nudged her out into the alley, and closed the door.

CHAPTER 15

Rosa stood pressed against the door. Dozens of doleful-eyed alien costumes continued to float past her. The wind puffed them up like balloons. The sight could not have been better designed for Halloween.

Even the streetlight at the end of the alley seemed to have been planned as part of the scene. It cast an eerie glow on the green aliens as they swept by. Had the town drunk seen the sight he might have thought an alien UFO had landed and the invasion of earth had begun. The war of the worlds had started, just as Orson Wells had once announced.

Rosa waited as the last of the costumes floated up into the night sky to be greeted by a full moon. Hundreds of little green men outlined against the moon. A weird sight. Moon madness.

But this is Roswell, thought Rosa. And this madness is real. Saytir is real.

She knew that every July Roswell celebrated its annual UFO festival. It drew visitors from all over the world: believers, skeptics, con men, trinket vendors, Germans, and an assortment of writers peddling their books. Aliens were big business for the city. The chamber of commerce loved the business the festival created, but what they didn't know was that tonight, somewhere in their fair city, lurked a present and real danger.

But why did Nadine send me to the car? Rosa wondered. Why would she take a chance and go back into the room where Saytir had appeared? What did she mean when she said that Saytir *wanted* her? Have I been set up? Is Nadine part of the conspiracy? No, I know better. Ed is dead. I saw his corpse. Himits tried to grab me in Santa Fe. Nadine shot and killed a strange creature.

The thoughts troubled her. Something wasn't right. Something hadn't been right all along. That's why she had to question everything, including Nadine. Too many things just didn't add up. What in the hell was she supposed to do with the explosives? Even if there was a message on the CD about how to use them, she was *not* going to blow up anything. And who was Marcy? Could she be trusted? Could anyone, including Nadine, be trusted?

She wished she had her cell phone. Call Bobby. Get some help. She was deep into a plot gone insane. Was it true that Saytir and his mad scientists wanted the DNA of the ChupaCabra she had met aboard the cruise ship? José and Chuco, two trusted friends, had been killed by the ChupaCabra. Their skulls had been punctured, their brains turned to mush. Both had been drug users. Was there a connection? She had touched them both. Could she be carrying the DNA Saytir wanted? Where was it? On her? On the clothes she wore that day? Or absorbed into her skin as Nadine suggested?

She shivered. No time to stand around and hope for easy answers. They did want to kill her, of that she was sure. And now she had to make her escape in a car packed with explosives. In the current terrorist scare that was sweeping the country just being in the car would get her whisked off to Guantanamo. According to the Patriot Act *anyone* could be made to disappear—if the government said so. Habeas corpus, the most basic protection for the common citizen, had been thrown out the window.

Was the country headed in the direction of the recent Latin American dictators who had *disappeared* thousands who opposed them? The killing fields of Salvador came to mind. Argentina came to mind. Others. Would the same tactics be used here? Rosa wondered.

She turned down the alley, then stopped short. A man stood at the end of the alley. A shadow she recognized as the one of the clones who had attacked her in Santa Fe. A himit. She turned to flee, but at the other end stood another himit. As they came toward her their human masks fell away. They were taking their ChupaCabra forms. In the dark their eyes burned red, laser-like.

Rosa gasped. She reached for the small cross hanging around her neck. In the Old World the cross could turn away the evil nature of vampires and werewolves. But that was in a universe where common rules of faith were shared. Even Dracula and werewolf had human forms, and they lived in a Christian world. They were subject to that power of good emanating from the cross. That's how the old legends were composed. There had to be a power greater than the beasts of the night. Else human life might not be tolerable.

But that was in the past. What now closed in on Rosa were clones, beasts constructed in laboratories, alien DNA mixed with ChupaCabra DNA. These creatures knew nothing of the spirituality that was inherent in the world's religions. Himits respected no belief system, no faith, no god. Synthetic biology gone wild. Monsters far more threatening than Frankenstein now walked the earth. They could not be turned away by prayer. They were controlled by C-Force, and maybe even C-Force no longer controlled the himits. Nadine had hinted that Saytir was now the controller. He was commander-in-chief of the conspiracy. The Decider. The evil created by C-Force had arrived, and once it took what it wanted from Rosa, everything else would fall.

"You can't escape!" one of the himits called, his voice crackling with a static that disturbed even the communication satellites far above the earth. The beasts were advancing to devour the lamb.

Ice flooded her veins. They knew they had her trapped. Moments ago she could have relied on her speed and run, but the alley was blocked.

She had to act.

This is not new, she thought. I've been stalked before. The ChupaCabra on the cruise ship had come after her, and she had fought back. Adrenaline coursed through her blood, flooded her brain, filled her lungs, made every muscle quiver. An ancient instinct inherited from the past told her that her will to survive was intact.

She could knock on the door, hope Nadine heard and opened it. But there wasn't time for that, and besides, Nadine had her hands full. Rosa knew she was on her own and she had to fight.

Just as the himits rushed at her Rosa leaped on the trash bin, reached up, grabbed the fire escape ladder, and climbed.

The himits scrambled after her and, as she neared the roof, one of the himits grabbed her leg. Rosa kicked hard and her heel caught the himit on the face. It shrieked and fell back, striking the second himit. Both fell to the ground below.

Rosa clambered onto the roof, ran to the front of the museum, and looked down. She had no choice but to jump.

"Blessed Mary," she whispered. Would the huge banner advertising the museum break her fall? If it didn't, she might break her neck on the sidewalk below. Behind her the two himits had already jumped onto the roof.

Taking a deep breath, Rosa grabbed the banner and jumped. She went sliding down, burning her hands but landing safely on the sidewalk.

Without looking back she raced to the car and started it. Before she could put it into gear a fist crashed through the window, revealing a claw-like hand reaching for her throat.

Rosa stepped on the gas, heard the screams of the himit as she dragged it down the dark street, then a loud thump as it fell away.

Heart racing, she sped away, gunning the car for all it was

worth. She needed a place to hide. Where? She knew no one in Roswell. The police couldn't be trusted. Where could she turn? Who could she trust?

Nadine had said to find Marcy. A librarian. Of what use was a librarian?

CHAPTER 16

When in trouble, head for a truck stop. Truckers can be trusted. Hardworking messengers who carry goods across the country. So they get a little wild once in a while, who doesn't? Was it Willie Nelson who wrote them a ballad? Or was it Johnny Cash? His "I've Been Everywhere" suited truckers.

I'll find food and a phone there, thought Rosa as she peered into the dark.

Around her Roswell slept. Hardworking people, minding their own business, paying their taxes, educating their kids, taking care of their community. They attended church, held the Bible close to their hearts, organized baseball and football leagues for the kids. Kind people, neighborly, trying to put the intolerance of the past behind them, dreaming the American dream.

They knew nothing of Ed's murder and the sinister plot that had placed him in a glass case in the museum. When their kids visited the museum they would be told Ed was just a joke. A Doubter.

See what will happen to you, Junior. If you're a bad boy, the aliens will put you in a glass case. There's no escaping.

The aliens are going to get you is right, Rosa thought. Saytir's out to get all of you. The common day citizens of Roswell knew nothing of the conspiracy that C-Force was hatching in their backyard.

But where was the laboratory? And what resources did Saytir need for such a vast project? Was it true, as Nadine said, that some of the clones were now members of the police force and the city government? If so, there was something rotten in Roswell.

A car passed her on the dark, deserted streets. Rosa caught a glimpse of two nurses on their way to work. A refuse truck turned a corner, workers getting ready to pick up the city's garbage. They would have a hell of a time gathering the alien costumes the wind had scattered.

Slowly, the city would awaken. The wind was dying down. Time for spring chores. Once the sun rose housewives would be out pruning rosebushes, planting backyard tomatoes, making sure the lawn was cut. At the local barbershops and coffee shops basketball aficionados would be comparing team scores. Some would attend the state basketball tournaments. New Mexico, like the rest of the nation, was caught up in March madness. From small towns to big-time colleges, basketball was king.

How ordinary, thought Rosa. How much I would love to be in that ordinary time. Instead I'm driving around in a car carrying enough explosives to put a big hole in Roswell. Separated from Nadine. And only Nadine knew the plan.

Dammit, what plan? What do I do now? Call Bobby. The thought was on her mind. But Bobby was in L.A. He couldn't just rush to Roswell. And if he could come, it would take time. Time she didn't have. Something was going to happen in the next few hours. Something momentous. But she didn't know what.

Call home? Rosa, call home. She heard her father's voice. Both parents always reminding her to call home. She knew if she called him, her father would get in his car and come in an instant. And her mother. But did she want them involved in the danger? No. She had to solve the mess herself. She had to get to Marcy.

With these thoughts tumbling through her mind Rosa pulled into a truck stop. She parked the car in a dark place where it might not be noticed and hurried inside.

Two truckers sat at a table, shoveling down eggs, bacon, pancakes with lots of butter, and cupfuls of coffee. Roswell acid.

A loner sat at the counter reading a newspaper. He glanced at Rosa. She sat and ordered coffee and a doughnut from the waitress. While being served she went to the bathroom, and on her way out she spotted a wall phone.

Rosa took a chance and dialed home. She would be waking up her parents but she wanted to assure them she was all right. It would be a lie, but she had to touch base. She heard the first ring, then the static. Barely audible, but it was there. Nadine would say a satellite in space was picking up her signal. Or a himit.

The man at the counter was looking at her.

Rosa quickly hung up the phone. Nadine had warned her. Saytir's himits were looking for her. The phone would be a dead giveaway.

She hurried to the counter to her coffee and doughnut. As she ate the low hum, the static, began again. From time to time the man glanced at her. Rosa recognized the eyes of a himit. He was reading her thoughts.

She choked on her coffee.

"You okay, honey?" the waitress asked in a Little Texas drawl.

Rosa nodded, paid the check, and hurried out. She could feel the stare of the himit through the glass pane. She turned right to make the clone think she was going in that direction, and when the himit could no longer see her through the window, she ran all the way around the truck stop to the car.

They're everywhere, she thought. What good would running around the truck stop do if they were tuning in to her?

Did she have something on her person that allowed them to locate her? The clone policeman's flashlight! She had stuck it in her jacket pocket. She took it out and threw it as far as she could. It made an arc in the light and then a thud when it landed.

Rosa looked at the car. Was there something else in the car that they might use to trace her? The explosives! She opened the trunk and looked at the packages. Plastic explosives, Nadine had said. Enough to blow a hole in Roswell. Enough for Ed's plan.

Next to the explosives was something covered with a tarp. She hadn't noticed it before. What was it? She pulled the tarp aside, revealing a black box with a small antenna. The box contained a clock. Illuminated red numbers, the digital seconds clicking away. She had seen enough terrorist movies to know the box was some kind of detonator wired to the explosives. The clock read six. The seconds were eating away the time, heading toward six. Was that when the car bomb would explode?

Rosa slammed the trunk shut.

"Damn, Nadine!" she shouted. "You double-crossed me!"

She couldn't run and leave the car. If it went off where it wasn't supposed to, a lot of innocent people would die.

She cursed again, got in the car, and drove away.

CHAPTER 17

Rosa drove into the dark streets of Roswell, not exactly a lost soul but feeling bereft. She was driving a car that didn't belong to her, one packed with explosives, she knew next to nothing about Nadine, or about Ed, for that matter.

She jogged her memory, trying to remember. Sights and sounds, images. High school. So long ago. Friends, teachers, classes, and in the background, Ed. He had asked her the prom; she said no. Didn't he know she was dating Larry? And why her? Ed was handsome, she remembered, but not popular with the girls. Why? He was shy and quiet, but other guys were shy and quiet. He was a bookworm. Straight A student. A loner. Girls didn't go for loners. He had transferred into Santa Fe High his senior year, so he hadn't grown up with her gang of kids. She knew everyone in school; Ed knew no one.

She wished now she had paid more attention. He had sought her out, a lonely creature trying to communicate. After that he blurred into the background. She heard he had gone to college.

Did he harbor a resentment? Had he returned to draw her into his conspiracy? Was Nadine part of the plan? What was the plan?

She peered into the dark. She didn't know anyone in Roswell, the cops couldn't be trusted, the clones were all around, and she couldn't phone Bobby.

She laughed. "And Saytir wants to kill me," she said aloud. "Don't forget that. Saytir wants your skin because he believes you have the ChupaCabra's DNA."

Well, he's not going to get it, she resolved. When the going gets tough, a woman gets tougher. I gotta find Marcy.

Roswell wasn't big. A quiet town sitting on the llano of southeastern New Mexico. There was a big industrial park south of town, a branch college, the military school, new businesses sprouting. Then there was Cannon Air Force Base near Portales. Flyboys roamed the local watering places, looking for cowgirls with nothing but time on their hands.

Not much to recommend it, thought Rosa, but don't tell that to the chamber of commerce boosters. As every man's home is his castle, every hometown is *home*, and don't knock it.

It's true, Rosa thought, New Mexico was a hardscrabble place. There was shining tourism in Santa Fe, lots of federal bucks in Los Alamos, gas and oil up in Farmington and down around Hobbs, air force bases in a few cities, the Spaceport America near Alamogordo, and a booming housing market as more people moved into the sunny climate. Still, most small towns struggled to get by.

Every small town was into growth. Not to grow and prosper was to die. An organic principle laid over inert life. The American Dream. To invite tourism dollars the town boosters invented tourist attractions. Tourism was a big industry. Clean. Tourists came, looked, and went away. Some stayed. That was the problem with tourism.

Boosterism was alive and well in the small town psyche, thought Rosa. But sooner or later I'll be spotted. Or stopped by the police.

Suddenly there it was. The Roswell library. And in the dark, standing by the door, a figure waving frantically.

Rosa stepped on the gas. Damn! Someone had seen her! She drove away, then had second thoughts. The figure waving for her to stop was a woman. Not Saytir.

Could it be? she thought. She drove around the block and stopped in front of the library. If it was a trap this was the end. If the figure waving at her was Marcy, maybe there was help.

She rolled down the window.

The woman asked, "You're Rosa?"

"Yes. You're Marcy?"

"Yes. Come in."

"I need to park the car where it won't be spotted."

"Park around the back. I'll open the door."

Rosa drove around the back and parked. At the back door she was greeted by Marcy, a librarian's librarian: old-fashioned to the bun on her head, large round glasses, and a baggy dress that gave away nothing of her figure.

"I'm so glad you're here," Marcy gushed, out of breath.

Rosa remained cautious. "How did you know I'd be here?"

"I know the timetable," Marcy replied. "Did they get Nadine?"

"I don't know. We split up at the museum—"

"Never mind. Come this way."

She led Rosa through a labyrinth of stacks to a dimly lit office. Not meticulous. The room was piled high with files, books, papers, notebooks, stacks of newspapers yellow with age. On a desk in the corner sat a computer, almost hidden behind more stacks of papers. Images of UFOs flew back and forth on the monitor.

"I love history," Marcy explained. "Of course I'm not a regular librarian. I sneak in and work at night. Which I love. I'm a night person. And tonight is the most important night of my life. The cusp of the spring equinox, you know."

Rosa looked around the small, cluttered office. Origami, wind chimes, alien drawings, photos of UFOs, reports on sightings, the Socorro find where Gehrman swore a UFO had crashed and baked the earth, more piles of books, and a stuffed goat.

"The goat?"

"The only animal known to have been killed by a UFO," Marcy explained. "Ain't it sweet?"

Rosa didn't brother to ask about what looked like an extraterrestrial decomposing in a glass case.

"Messy, I know, but I like it that way. So, welcome to Roswell. And our library, the pride of our town. We have every book that's ever been written about the alien invasion." She smiled.

Rosa almost laughed. Welcome to Roswell? She was being hunted by Saytir and all Marcy could say was *welcome to Roswell*?

"Thank you."

"I know you're tired. And a terrible thing has happened. But you're safe here. Can I get you a glass of water? We have wonderful water in Roswell."

Rosa nodded. As she drank she thought: this woman is not going to be much help.

"Saytir. You know about Saytir?"

"Oh, yes. I know everything. Well, almost everything."

"He attacked us at the museum . . ."

"Probably. But don't worry, you're safe here."

"Safe?"

"Saytir can't harm us here. He can't enter."

"What do you mean he can't enter?"

Marcy shrugged. "The library is a sanctuary. Like a church or synagogue. Or a mosque. Or a kiva." She smiled. "I like that. You know our Indian neighbors have kivas. For their ceremonies." She seemed satisfied with her answer.

Rosa shook her head. "What do you mean?"

"Well, the aliens that landed are not evil. And neither are ChupaCabras. It's the way men use those creatures that's evil."

Rosa nodded. She had a point. The original aliens, if there were such a thing, might have been a group of space wayfarers just looking for a place to have dinner. The Argonauts of space. Harmless. And the ChupaCabra was a creature in many world legends.

But now Saytir and his mad scientists were mixing the DNA of two creatures never before seen on earth.

CHAPTER 18

"You don't understand," Rosa complained. "The car is loaded with explosives, and there's a clock ticking. I'm sure the thing is set to explode at 6 a.m. Or p.m. I don't know."

"Probably," Marcy replied, somewhat distracted. "It's part of the plan!" she beamed, as if she knew something.

"Ed's plan?"

"Yes, of course."

"So what do I do?"

"Oh, I don't know the plan. We have to wait for Nadine. Ed took it with him."

"But Ed's dead. Stuffed. I mean in a glass case at the museum."

"Terrible, terrible. But Nadine will take care of things. Ed will destroy Saytir's evil empire. Ed was kind of like a saint, you know. Even though I'm not religious in that way."

Rosa shook her head. When Nadine told her to look up Marcy she had expected to find a woman as tough as Nadine. But Marcy wasn't going to be of much help. Should she stay or take her chances out on the street, looking for Nadine?

"You said alien invasion. Do you really believe that aliens from outer space landed here, crashed here, in 1947?"

"Oh yes. Our brethren have been coming to earth for a long time. Let me show you something." Marcy took a dusty folder and opened it. "My compilation," she said proudly.

Rosa looked at the pictures. Aliens in space uniforms, discs flying through gloomy skies, dragons, petroglyphs that showed humanlike figures with helmets, Stonehenge, Machu Picchu, Quetzalcoatl dragon faces on the pyramids of Teotihuacán. Faun like figures. Bigfoot. The Abominable Snowman. Red Riding Hood's big bad wolf. Circles and other designs cut into English cornfields. Hundreds more.

"These are aliens?"

"Mysteries. One theory says our brethren have built colonies at the bottom of the sea. The Dragon Triangle. What do you think?"

Rosa shook her head. "There are hundreds of theories—"

Marcy nodded. "True. The humans just haven't figured it out, have they?"

"Are you saying aliens are real?"

Marcy looked hurt. "Of course they are. I spent years documenting them. Ed helped. He knows more about our brethren than anyone. You know, sometimes I got the feeling that Ed was one of them." She puckered her lips and closed her eyes in thought.

Rosa remembered what Uncle Billy had said. The people from space had been coming to earth for a long time. Had they taken on human form? Did they walk among us? Are we related to those space travelers? Were the huge advances in science and knowledge that different civilizations experienced from time to time due to aliens from the Pleiades? Did a spaceship lift the prophet Elijah up into the sky?

"No," Rosa said. She couldn't let go of her humanism, the belief that what was done on earth was all of human invention. "No," she repeated. "What we do, we do."

"Ah, don't be too sure," Marcy replied, opening her eyes. "I'm an expert. The constellations are my specialty. I just love them. From Pegasus to Andromeda, they've all been documented. Here on earth astronomers are just discovering the Gliese 876 system. Finding sunlike stars surrounded by planets, like Epsilon Eridani and Tau Ceti, and the NASA satellite mission to detect exoplanets, the Terrestrial Planet Finder . . . oh dear, I fear I'm getting ahead of myself."

Rosa took a deep breath. "Let's get back to Ed. You think he was a—brethren, as you call them?"

"No, no. I was just thinking aloud. He knew so much. So sensitive. He was almost like Jesus. So kind, intelligent." She poked a Kleenex under her glasses and wiped away tears. "And they crucified him."

Rosa waited for Marcy to compose herself.

"But the police? They have to file a report—"

"Don't you know they'll just blame it on Mexican immigrants. The country's blaming them for everything. Or blame the rednecks. We have plenty of those."

Marcy pointed at the dusty folders on the shelves. "I've gathered just about all the history of this area: genealogies, the homesteaders, the air force bases, the dairy industry—did you smell that cow smell? Comes right over us when the wind is right. The Goodnight-Loving Trail. They weren't Hollywood cowboys, you know. Just plain boys who took care of cows. They learned a lot about rodeoing from the Mexican vaqueros. I've got volumes on the oil industry. It's ruining our environment. Earth, water, flora, and fauna. That's all we have, and we're destroying everything."

A conservationist who believes in extraterrestrials, thought Rosa. What a combination. Were all Roswellians spacey?

"I know the people who have made money pumping oil," Marcy continued. "If I were to publish what I know, even the president's head might roll." She paused. "That might not be such a bad idea.

But I'm just a collector. I don't publish. And the oil industry does give the library small contributions from time to time. To keep us quiet. The Ogallala aquifer is drying up, you know. I have collected items on Billy the Kid even the best scholars haven't seen. I know where he's really buried," she whispered conspiratorially.

The yellow papers were crumbling in the folders.

"Has anyone read your collections?" asked Rosa.

Marcy looked at her like a puppy lost in a snowstorm. "People hardly read anymore. Isn't it a shame? Kids have their video games. Parents are too busy. Students from the college do their research on the Internet. We're a dying breed, Rosa. May I call you Rosa? Such a pretty name."

"Of course." Rosa nodded. Marcy wasn't so strange after all. Rosa knew college students resisted reading. One could get a PhD without ever having visited a library. Internet/instant knowledge. Marcy had collected the history of the entire east side of the state, but no one was coming to the store.

"Hoopla," Marcy said. "They come to the UFO festival, but not to the library. The children do come to reading hour. But they grow up and we never see them again."

Rosa felt herself being sucked into Marcy's stories. A sweet lady with a very intense way of communicating. But there were other priorities calling.

"Nadine. And the explosives in the car."

Marcy looked at her as if she had just walked into the room. "Did she tell you about the genome project?"

"No."

"You know about the human genome project?"

Rosa searched her mental files. During the Clinton years science had finally mapped the entire human gene sequence. A major breakthrough. Now science was working to identify specific genes. Soon the gene networks responsible for many human diseases would be identified, and then individual genes or their networks could be manipulated to produce cures. Cure Parkinson's, cancer, obesity, and diabetes. Mix genes and produce new combinations. Women could elect to give birth to a boy or a girl, order color of eyes, height, IQ, personality . . . genetic engineering gone wild.

"Cloning?"

"Yes. They cloned sheep, mice, dogs. The next step is to clone a person. A human being."

"What does this have to do with Saytir and C-Force?"

"Saytir's labs are completing the ChupaCabra genome. They may already have completed it."

Rosa's mind spun. She reached for the edge of a table to steady herself. Marcy's talking science fiction, she thought. It had to be science fiction. But in her heart she knew the advances of gene science were progressing exponentially. Ethics were being left behind.

"The ChupaCabra genome," she whispered, almost laughing. "Not possible."

"Believe me, it's not just possible, it's a given," Marcy replied. "They decoded the genome of the brethren. They're almost ready to mix the two. Create a completely new creature. Not by God. Not by natural evolution. Beasts from the laboratories. Hundreds of them. Millions!"

CHAPTER 19

Rosa had been reading *Discover* magazine. She knew that every day brought astonishing new findings in gene theory. The twenty-four chromosomes were giving up their genetic secrets. The proteins in which they floated were being revealed, and also the life functions they performed.

"Here's what Ed was working on," Marcy whispered. "What if it's discovered that the ChupaCabra genome is nearly identical to the human genome? How far back in the evolutionary chain are we related? Is the ChupaCabra a divergent species? A kind of Neanderthal? An experiment of evolution related to humans? Did a colony of ChupaCabras disappear in the evolutionary ladder only to reappear in the mountains of Puerto Rico? And if they existed there, they could be in other places."

"A divergent species?" Rosa shook her head. "A species related to us? Alive?"

"Yes. A lost colony of hominids living in the isolated mountains of Puerto Rico. *Chupa-erectus puertoricos* Ed called it. Ed could have used its DNA to trace it back in time. To establish the relationship.

Instead Saytir's biologists and the government project took it and turned it into a monster."

A lost colony, Rosa thought. Absolutely incredible.

She looked at Marcy. The librarian was deep into some evolutionary theory, proposed by Ed, to try to explain ChupaCabras. Wasn't the recent appearance of ChupaCabras just a story, an urban legend composed by people trying to explain dead chickens in their backyards?

No, ChupaCabras were real. She had met at least one aboard a cruise ship. But what if what she had seen was not an original, but a clone? One whose DNA had been tampered with?

"Puerto Rico was the ChupaCabras' Easter Island," Marcy explained. "Isolated all those years . . ."

"I was attacked in Santa Fe by two clones Nadine called himits. Then by Saytir. Haven't they already accomplished what they set out to do?"

"Oh no," Marcy replied. "They created himits, all right, and they devised some kind of skin so they look human. Underneath that skin lurk the himits."

"They're dangerous."

"You better believe it."

"What now?"

"The first himits didn't have the right mixtures of DNA. They were early experiments. There aren't very many, and they're going to die off. The death gene, you know."

Rosa shook her head. Death gene? There was no such thing. Or was there?

"I don't know—" Rosa said. This was just too bizarre. But stranger things were happening in DNA experiments. She didn't know the science so she felt at a loss. Who really understood what was going on in the realm of DNA experimentation? Not the common citizen. Not laypeople. Not the hardworking Jacks and Janes just trying to make a living and raise families. Not her, Rosa Medina, who had a

PhD and had read most of contemporary Chicana/o literature, a lot of mythology and legends, but who knew little about genes, the carriers of hereditary messages.

What is a gene? The word had become commonplace. It was used to explain so many things. "I'm fat, it's my genes." "I'm good at math, must be my math gene." "My father lived to be ninety-nine, I have great longevity genes." On and on. Everyone using a word they don't understand.

"The genome?" she asked.

"Come here." Marcy led her to the computer and typed.

Beautiful worlds of DNA chains appeared, floating and twisting in a sea of blue, as they must have floated in an earlier ocean eons ago. Proteins. Chemical nucleotide bases ACTG. Coalescing. The earliest cells. In each cell written the history of the species.

"There!" Marcy beamed. "The ChupaCabra genome."

Rosa looked closely. Band after band of unintelligible stuff scrolled down the screen into virtual non-reality.

"We hacked their computers. If they knew I had this they would kill me."

"Is this why they killed Ed?"

Marcy nodded. "He's the one who found it. It's priceless. I really mean that. This is the ultimate alchemist's formula. The creation of a new form of life. Dictators would give billions for this. Billions. Entire civilizations would be wiped off the face of the earth to get this. And whoever owns the genome would rule the world forever."

Her voice had risen as she talked, and in the end it took on a sad note. "It has to be destroyed."

"Ed's plan."

"Yes. But we need to know the lab's location. Exactly. We don't want to hurt the innocent." She moved the mouse and a sky view of buildings appeared. "This is the industrial park south of the city. Somewhere in here are Saytir's labs."

Rosa's pursed lips let out a low whistle. "Then you know everything."

"No. We don't know the exact location. And we don't know how the DNA is incubated. Do they plan to use human eggs? They can't get that many. Ed thought they would use cow eggs—in vitro is too expensive—or have they found a new way to grow the himits? Apes, chimpanzees. The process begins here, but they could take the eggs to a lab somewhere in South America, or to Puerto Rico, or, for that matter, remain here."

In the flickering light of the computer screen Marcy's face had grown wizened, old with worry wrinkles. "Here's a copy of the DNA genome of the ChupaCabra and the brethren." She slipped the CD into Rosa's hand. "Now I erase the hard drive. Only you have it. Ed trusted you. He got you here. Guard it with your life."

Rosa felt her stomach churn. She now had possession of a CD inscribed with the genomes of the ChupaCabra and the Roswell alien. She shook her head, not knowing what to believe.

"What did Nadine give you?" Marcy asked.

Rosa reached in her pocket and handed her the CD from the Loretto Chapel.

Marcy held the CD like a baby. She slipped it into the computer and an image appeared onto the screen.

"That's it!" Marcy jumped up.

Rosa looked at the buildings on the screen. "What?"

"This building!" she pointed. "That's the lab!" She jotted the name and location of the building on a piece of paper and handed it to Rosa. "For Nadine."

CHAPTER 20

"Listen," Marcy whispered. "Do you hear them?"

"I hear something," Rosa replied.

"Why bless you, child. I thought only we could hear them."

". . . a low humming sound."

"They're here."

"Who?"

"The brethren. Come!"

Marcy grabbed Rosa's hand and led her out the back door. "There!"

She pointed at an array of slow-moving lights that flew over the budding treetops. Three, then seven, moving in perfect formation. Then suddenly they zoomed toward the northwest and disappeared over city hall and the post office building. The low hum Rosa had heard disappeared with them.

"Bless the brethren, they're here," Marcy whispered reverently, as if she had just witnessed the second coming.

"UFOs?"

"Oh no, dear. We know exactly what they are."

"But . . . right over the city. Why?" Rosa asked, shivering in the cool of the March night.

"Saytir wants us to believe there's nobody out there."

"Why?"

"He's afraid of them."

He censors their appearance? thought Rosa. Again *why* crossed her mind. Too many *whys*. Why was Saytir afraid? Why did Marcy say she knew who they were? Who is *they*?

What time is it, anyway? Rosa glanced at her watch. It had stopped the moment Nadine killed the cop/himit. The seventy-degree day had dropped to forty at night. A full moon shone in the starry sky. The first signs of spring were lingering in the air.

"Had you seen them before?" asked Marcy.

"When we drove into town."

"Most people can't see them. Like they can't see the Marfa lights. But you are sensitive enough to hear them. No wonder Ed found you. How silly of me. You were never missing."

"I don't know why Ed found me," Rosa replied. "I hardly knew him. I knew him in high school, that's all. I hardly remember him. Why me?" She didn't wait for an answer. "And those lights. Maybe they're just falling stars. A meteorite shower. Or weather balloons, or—"

She stopped short. With Nadine and now with Marcy it seemed that every time she turned around she was deeper and deeper into a fantastic world. Fantasy. Non-reality. She didn't believe in flying saucers. UFOs. What did brethren mean in Spanish? Family. *Familia*. Did Marcy mean the extraterrestrials were family from outer space? Primos, cousins.

She laughed softly. "Our primos."

She didn't feel related to aliens from space. Her familia was New Mexican. Ancestors from Santa Fe. Familia meant the Medinas, Ortegas, Pinos, Chavezes, the extended family. Raza. Fiestas where everyone showed up. Matanzas. Tierra. Calabacitas con maíz simmering in cream. Green chile guisado con cebollita. Acequias gurgling and watering corn. Big sky over the Sangre de Cristos. Deep faith. Pueblo dances. Grounded. Space was for the stars. Heaven. Constellations. God. Mystery.

Mystery? Had Marcy said there existed a lost colony of Chupa-Cabras hidden in the mountains of Puerto Rico? Little creatures who stood upright like Homo sapiens? Hidden for a million years? Did hunger drive them into the villages where they tasted the blood of goats? Is that how they became the goat suckers? Goat blood, chicken blood.

Aren't we also bloodsuckers? Meat eaters? How are we so different from ChupaCabras? Some cultures are known to eat dogs. The Donner party trapped in a High Sierra snowstorm turned to cannibalism. Why do some ideas seem so far-fetched, and yet so close to the heart?

"If the ChupaCabra genome is like the human one, or close to it, then . . . it is possible . . . we are . . ." Rosa was thinking aloud and the thoughts were disturbing.

Marcy reached out and touched her. Her hands were cold. Rosa looked into the shining eyes of the woman who believed in the possibility of other worlds. All adventurers believed in other worlds. That's why they set out into the unknown: to see.

The religions of the world also believed in other worlds. The Good, the True, and the Beautiful. Ideal forms. A Divine Mind. God. Hades. Olympus. Heaven. Hell. Nirvana. Metempsychosis. Transmigration. Plans for the salvation of the soul. And the body. The Rapture. Everyone floating up, except the nonbelievers. They stayed behind.

But all the concepts are human inventions, thought Rosa. She was a skeptic, a rational person molded by her education. Western civilization trusted in the rational. It didn't have room for flying saucers. Don't trust what you can't see, count, weigh, or repeat in the laboratory as an experiment.

But she wasn't a scientist. She was a lover of literature, a lover of stories and legends, fascinated by the stories people had composed and told through the ages, interested in the projections of the psyche, the monsters from Cyclops to Grendel to Dracula to ChupaCabra. Characters in stories who became real. Why couldn't she believe in aliens from outer space? Their stories also had been composed by humans.

"I want to believe," she whispered, and her voice was lost in the breeze that moaned through the trees and bushes that did not hear her—their main intent at the moment was to push sap up from their roots to create the buds and leaves of spring. March madness. Nature was in full swing. Basketball was in full swing. The meaning of life was hanging on the budding elm trees. Perhaps the meaning of life was also being discussed in the interiors of the UFOs that had just buzzed Roswell.

"Ed knew you were special. That's why he trusted you. He loved you. That's why he sent Nadine to bring you here. I know it must seem terribly confusing to you . . . and dear child, you don't have to believe. You just have to do what is right."

Rosa wiped her eyes, ashamed to think tears had sprouted there. She nodded. "Why are they here? The brethren?"

"'They've always been here. Don't you see, they've been watching over us. Like God's angels. Yes, think of the brethren as angels. Watching over earth these millions of years. From time to time they take a human up into their spaceship to be with them. They mean no harm. They just want to know if Homo sapiens are becoming better human beings."

"But what's their interest in us? Aren't there hundreds of other planets out there?" Rosa waved at the starry sky.

"Oh yes," Marcy gushed, "but earth is special. From the very beginning, when they first started observing earth, they knew it was a special place. The universe is so vast you can't begin to comprehend it, and yet once they found this little planet lost in space they wrote in their star maps that earthlings were destined to do great things."

She paused. "They were right. Think of the music and literature, art, science, math, great buildings, conquered diseases . . . and everything is documented and saved in libraries. I think the day they decide to land they'll come to the libraries first. Won't that be a treat. Imagine all the kids running to the library to meet the brethren. Reading books would be back in style."

"Yes," Rosa said, "but they will also find the books on the wars we created, pogroms, the Holocaust, the millions killed in the name of king or president or religion. Darfur, the starving children, the greed, weapons that have destroyed civilizations, nuclear war—"

She stopped and stared at Marcy. A light shimmered in the dark and illuminated Marcy's tired face.

"Oh dear. Yes. You're right. The good has to be balanced with the bad, and if evil outweighs the good, they will destroy us."

"Do you *really* believe that?"

"They're like angels, aren't they? They have helped in the past. When humans get out of hand they step in and make things right. Look at history. All those times we thought the world would end and they set it right. But if things get too out of hand, well . . ."

"Is that why they're here now?"

"Why yes. Didn't Ed tell you? We either destroy Saytir's evil project or they will. Believe me, if they do, it will be the end of the world. We have to go!" she exclaimed, pulling Rosa toward the car.

CHAPTER 21

"I can't go anywhere without Nadine!" Rosa protested.

Marcy tightened her hold on Rosa's wrist. "We don't have time! They'll be gone!"

"Who will be gone?" Rosa cried, pulling free.

"The brethren!"

"The spaceships? They're already gone! They disappeared!"

"No, they're here! Ed predicted they would come! Didn't he tell you?"

"No, Ed didn't tell me anything! I've gotten deeper and deeper into this—and I know nothing."

"I'm sorry, I'm sorry," Marcy said. "I thought you knew Ed's predictions. They're landing tonight. We *must* be there!"

"Those lights, the UFOs—you believe they're landing?" Rosa shook her head. Things were spinning out of control, but they had been since Nadine rescued her from the two—himits. Clones. Saytir. Whatever!

"Of course they're landing! That's why I was waiting for you.

Ed planned everything down to the last detail. Of course fate interferes in our plans, but we have to go on."

"And you want me to take you there?"

"Why yes. That's why you're here."

"I shouldn't be driving anywhere!" Rosa protested. "There are explosives in the car, a clock ticking away, Nadine's gone, and if the cops catch me with—"

"You have no choice," Marcy said and pointed. A car had just pulled up. Two himits alighted, and as they did the car's interior light illuminated Saytir's face, sitting in the back seat, staring at Rosa and Marcy the way a snake stares at a bird before it strikes.

Marcy looked back at the library. "Oh dear, I hate to leave all my research behind. I only hope a librarian will come along and take up where I left off."

That said, she opened the car door and pushed Rosa inside, "Drive!" she shouted.

A shocked Rosa said the first words of a prayer, started the car, and thought, is this the end of the line?

"Drive!" Marcy repeated.

Rosa pressed the accelerator and gunned the car straight at one of the clones. The impact sent himit catapulting over the car.

"One down!" Marcy shouted.

"Yeah," Rosa agreed. She wasn't about to give up without a fight. She drove straight at Saytir's car and turned, narrowly missing it. Sparks flew as the car jumped the curb and scraped the street.

"Good!" Marcy shouted encouragement, then added, "Oh this is divine!"

Rosa raced past the federal building. She glanced at her rearview mirror. Saytir's car was following.

"Where to?"

"Turn right on Main!" Marcy shouted, grabbing the steering wheel and pulling.

"Let me drive!" Rosa pushed her away.

"Sorry, sorry, oh what excitement!"

Rosa frowned. Damn, this is not about excitement, this is about survival.

"We're safe."

"Not exactly," Rosa replied.

Shots rang out. Marcy pointed and shouted encouragement and Rosa drove like she had never driven before.

"Turn here! Turn here!" Marcy cried and Rosa complied, zigzagging in and out of downtown streets and alleys. With the accelerator pressed to the floor, she finally lost them. Or they had merely pulled back to give her rope to hang herself. After all, Saytir controlled much of the city; he could bide his time. They could identify the car. It was all a matter of time; she knew that.

"Okay," she said, glancing in the rearview mirror, feeling her sweating hands gripping the steering wheel. "For a while."

"Wonderful, Rosa, wonderful! You are a brave woman. I feel, I feel . . . oh, exhilarated!"

"Now what?"

"You know about the 1947 crash? Near Corona—"

"I know. But we're not going there, are we? That's an hour drive. I have to find Nadine and get rid of this car." She glanced at Marcy and swore she had never seen a more serene face.

"We're not going to the Corona site. That's old hullabaloo. The brethren have been landing everywhere in this area. In Santa Rosa, where by the way they landed by Hidden Lake and scared the pants off some boys fishing. One of the Delgado boys reported that in the local paper. I have a complete file on it. Oh dear, I had. Anyway, they have landed around Vaughn. And all along the Pecos River. The river is a Sun Line. Remember the story of the Golden Carp? It becomes a sun and floats up to the heavens. The author knew about the Sun Lines. He got it right."

"But he didn't write about UFOs."

"Read between the lines," Marcy replied.

Okay, Rosa nodded. When and if I get out of this I'm going to read everything again. Between the lines.

Rosa believed in the sacred meridians of the earth. From Stonehenge to the pyramids of Giza to Machu Picchu to the Alhambra, the Pyramid of the Sun, Chichén Itzá, the Taj Mahal, humans had raised temples along the meridians. The Sun Lines. The body also had its meridians, discovered by the Chinese long ago and used in acupuncture. Many ancient cultures believed the body was analogous to the earth. The entire universe was imprinted on the body's nerves, brain, muscles, tendons. Sun Lines.

"They land along the Sun Lines? Is that it?" Rosa was struggling to understand, to believe.

"Yes, but they can land anywhere. They have hovered right above Roswell, but they prefer the desert where the earth is not profaned by men."

"Profaned?"

"You know, humans have destroyed most of the earth. From the Amazon forest to the melting ice caps. The brethren look for desolate spots where the energy of the Sun Lines is pure."

"So where do we go?"

"Just past Verbena Road we'll turn. Take some ranch roads. I just hope we're in time."

In time for what, thought Rosa. At least they weren't being followed, and the explosives hadn't gone off, and Marcy, who had enjoyed the chase, obviously knew where she was going.

They drove in silence until Marcy pointed. "There's the ranch road. Turn there."

Rosa turned the car down a narrow dusty road. The headlights illuminated flat scrub country. Desert. No irrigated fields. From time to time a lone steer appeared off the side of the road. The washboard road was bumpy, probably used only by ranchers, the land desolate.

"I've been thinking," Rosa said, "about cloning. Wasn't Dolly the sheep, the first clone, incubated in the mother sheep?"

"That's only the first cloning the government told the people about."

"There were others before that?"

"Yes. Part of the C-Force conspiracy. Keep the people ignorant. There are all sorts of eggs they can use. Cow eggs for example. We have large dairies in the Roswell and Portales area. Thousands of cows. They can take the genetic material out of a cow egg and insert the ChupaCabra/alien DNA. That simple."

The idea made Rosa queasy. The thought of cows giving birth to Saytir's monsters was revolting.

Marcy was concentrating on the dark sky overhead, searching for the lights.

"In a couple of movies I saw," Rosa continued, "the bodies are grown in sacs. Sacs filled with fluid. There are usually huge underground laboratories—"

"Nonsense," Marcy said. "Hollywood hullabaloo. I think they're going to use cows, the perfect mammal. I've seen those sci-fi movies. Ed loved movies. He and I and Nadine would be up all night watching movies and eating popcorn." She sighed. "I will miss those days. But the laboratories with the sacs, that's baloney. They give those movie directors in Hollywood too much poetic license."

"And the brethren?" Rosa asked. "Do they look like those little men with big round heads and almond eyes, like the one in the alien autopsy?"

"That's a bunch of crock," Marcy replied. "They look just like—"

She stopped short and shouted, "There!"

Out of the dark sky appeared a light, then seven, and the humming sound.

"Glory be," she whispered. "We're on time!"

CHAPTER 22

In the starry sky the lights came hovering toward them in perfect formation, illuminating the desert below.

Rosa heard the low humming sound. She turned to Marcy. Marcy's face was ecstatic.

"My oh my, aren't they beautiful," she whispered.

Helicopters, thought Rosa. The police have found us out, reported us, and now a SWAT team is arriving from Cannon Air Force Base. And there is no way in hell that this car is going to outrun them. Jail time, mi'jita.

The lights grew brighter. One broke formation and came toward them, like a full moon over Roswell, a magnificent sight.

"Oh Lord, they're not helicopters," Rosa whispered.

"Of course not," Marcy replied. "The ships of the brethren."

Rosa looked up. The spaceship raised no dust as it neared. In fact, a sense of tranquility seemed to come over the desert. A few steers standing nearby did not seem to notice the huge disc descending.

Marcy turned to Rosa. "Thank you for everything. You're such a sweet girl. No wonder Ed was in love with you all those years.

And now you're entrusted with the future. I said earlier that fate dips its finger into our lives, but that's a cliché, isn't it? I've collected thousands of clichés over the years. Human language is full of clichés, and the truth is they can be wonderful metaphors. Anyway, what I really mean is that everything that happens has a purpose. Well, good-bye, Rosa."

She started to open the car door but Rosa grabbed her. "You're not going out there!"

By now the one craft loomed over them. Its silvery moon color had changed into a rainbow of lights.

"What is it!" Rosa shouted.

"I told you, child. The brethren. And I am going. Look."

The lights had grown so bright Rosa had to shield her eyes. The lights shone like a gigantic stained-glass window, a round mosaic outlined against the night sky. "A rose window," Rosa muttered. Whatever descended from the sky was a rose window. The strong blues and reds intimations of the window in the Chartres cathedral. Rosa expected to see the images of the Virgin and Child in the central rosette. But this was no work of man; this was the work of beings far beyond human comprehension. A world earthlings would never know.

"The brethren," Rosa whispered. The brethren were Argonauts from outer space. Or from some deep-sea colony as some believed. Marcy's family. *Familia*.

Her rational mind resisted believing what her eyes were recording. She did not want to believe that UFOs existed. But here was a disc in the shape of a rose window hovering over her, and the awe she felt dissolved her skepticism.

How could she not believe the brethren had landed in a rose ship far bigger and brighter and a thousand times more mysterious than anything on earth?

"Yes," Marcy said. "Now I must go." She took the bracelet from her wrist and handed it to Rosa. "Wear this for me. It's the last thing

I have on earth. Yes. I've left everything behind. Good-bye, Rosa."
She squeezed Rosa's hands and stepped out of the car.

"Good-bye," Rosa whispered. It all began to make some sort
of sense. Marcy had brought her to this place at this time. She had
known the ships would be here. Rosa's dread and fear began to
evaporate. She felt the same serene peace she had seen written on
Marcy's face.

The ship was a wonderful work of art. The brightness of the
lights grew dim, so now she could clearly see the true beauty of the
colorful mosaic. No show of neon light or Las Vegas casino lights
or New York City lights could compare with the huge rose ship.
The lights shone with a divine essence, far beyond earthly lights.
And the humming was now a kind of melody, not audible but sen-
sory. A music coursing through her body.

Marcy looked angelic walking toward the ship. A breeze teased
her skirt. She held it down like a young woman might bashfully
hold down her skirt on a Sunday picnic. She turned and waved.
Rosa waved back.

A circular staircase descended from the ship and Marcy began
to climb it with a confidence that suggested she had climbed that
staircase before. She was returning to something she knew quite
well. Then with a last wave good-bye she disappeared into the ship
and the staircase was withdrawn.

Rosa burst out crying. A great sadness welled up from her soul,
and she could not contain the sobs that came. She cried for Marcy
and for the miracle she had just witnessed. Later she would ask
herself if it had been an illusion, for the world, she knew, was full
of illusions. In the future she would recall the image of the huge
rose ship and feel thankful she had been a witness. Illusion or not,
there was just too much mystery in the universe not to believe.

She wiped her eyes and watched as the ship climbed quickly
into the sky to join the others. Then in formation they darted away
and were gone, leaving behind a silent vacuum.

Except for Marcy's disappearance and Rosa's emotions, nothing seemed disturbed by the arrival of the spaceships. The earth went on rotating, the full moon shone over Roswell, and the steers nearby went on chewing their cud. A jackrabbit bounded across the car's lights and a coyote followed. Life on earth went on.

Rosa slipped on the bracelet, a kind of supple metal with small, round balls on each end in the mosaic image of the rose ship. The bracelet looked like the kind people wear for arthritis, but far more intriguing and lovely. She felt a slight buzz from the bracelet. A communication. A field of energy seemed to flow from one of the nodules to the other. Marcy's thoughts?

Rosa smiled. "Time to kick ass, Nadine would say."

She had to find Nadine. Marcy had written down the building where Saytir had put together the genomes. Nadine needed that information.

Rosa started the car and backed into the dry grass stubble and yuccas on the side of the road. Then she drove away from the place, making her way along the ranch roads to the highway.

Once back in town there was only one place to look for Nadine. The UFO museum. Would Saytir be looking for Rosa or had he retired to his lair, the laboratory? And the police? Did they now have a description of the car? Would they be looking for her? It didn't matter. She was driving a beat-up, dusty car with the rear end almost scraping the ground, a trunk load of explosives, and—

And it was time to finish the mission.

The first faint light of dawn appeared as she drove down Main Street and turned into the museum alley. There waiting for her, almost if it had been planned, stood Nadine.

"Rosa, glad to see you, mujer. Help me." She pointed at a large bag.

Rosa got out of the car. "What is it?"

"Ed."

"Ed's in the bag?"

"I couldn't let those bastards keep him as a museum piece for people to laugh at. No way. He's going with me. Just like he always wanted."

"But—"

"We don't have time, Rosa. Come on."

She opened the back door of the car and picked up one end of the bag. Rosa picked up the other and together, pulling and pushing, they got the body in and closed the door.

"Marcy gave you the location of the building?"

Rosa dug in her pocket and handed Nadine the note.

"Great! Let's pull the trigger. You drive." She held her mangled arm out for Rosa to see.

CHAPTER 23

"What happened to your arm?"

"Himit . . ." She winced and laughed. "But you should see the himit."

Rosa looked at the mangled arm. "Looks bad. It's not bleeding?"

"It's okay, girl. Just drive. Or I can drive with one arm."

"No, I'll do it. Where to?" Rosa dared to ask, although by now she knew.

"The industrial park south of town—wait. You've done as much as you can. I can drive. Why don't I can drop you off at the bus depot. You can go home. This score's almost done."

"And miss the end? No way."

"You sure?"

"I'm all in."

"Royal flush! Vamos!"

She was trying to stay tough, but Rosa could tell the wound was serious. The arm looked like it had gone through a thresher, and Nadine's eyes were clouded. Whatever pain was like in her world, she was feeling it.

"Marcy's gone," Rosa said, unsure of what gone meant. Gone to the seven Pleiades? Gone with the brethren? Beings she knew? Beings that were family to her?

"Good for her," Nadine replied.

Rosa let out a nervous laugh. "The ship I saw, if that's what I saw, was in the shape of a giant rose window."

"Yes, I've seen them. Like those beautiful stained-glass windows in the cathedrals. Ed showed me pictures."

"I thought they would be plain, but this one was just fantastic. Customized the kids would say. A lowrider UFO—"

Nadine smiled. "I love it. A lowrider UFO. Marcy helped us a lot. She deserved the best."

"Helped you and Ed?"

"Who else is there? And helped you too. Don't you feel better for the experience?"

Rosa nodded. Yes, she felt better for having known Marcy, although briefly, and witnessing her departure was something she would never forget.

"I felt the spaceship was real. And now I wonder: what did I really see?"

"You saw what you believe you saw," Nadine said. "Take it or leave it. Ed planned all of this. Down to the last detail. Except this one."

Flashing lights and a siren told them police had spotted them.

"Saytir?"

"Whatever," Nadine replied. "Anda! Step on it!"

Rosa stepped on the gas pedal and coaxed all the speed she could get out of the car.

"Lose them!" Nadine cried. "There's no turning back!"

Rosa knew the car didn't have the speed to outrun the police car; her only chance was to outmaneuver them. She drove toward the golf course.

"Atta girl! Pura pistolera!" Nadine shouted. "Let's golf!"

At the New Mexico Military Institute Rosa cut across the golf course, careening around the holes, the back end dipping and tearing up grass.

"They won't follow," Nadine said, looking back.

The police car had stalled in a sand trap.

"Now let's do the relief route to 285. We can take Hobson into the industrial park. Damn, that was good."

Just then Nadine's phone rang. She looked at the screen. "Our friend Saytir."

"You going to answer?"

"Why not?"

"They can trace you."

Nadine shrugged. "Himit knows we're coming." She pushed the speaker button so Rosa could listen. "What do you want?"

"Want? Why, I want you to come back home. You know that's what I've always wanted. Come home."

"Home ain't safe," Nadine replied.

"Of course it's safe," Saytir intoned. "Nobody here is going to hurt you. Your friend, Rosa, can go back to Santa Fe and join her family. She's listening, isn't she? You hear, Rosa? You can go home. No one will bother you."

"You attacked her in Santa Fe."

"That was a mistake."

"Your mistake?"

"Yes, I admit it. But if you come home she won't be bothered. I swear."

"You need the DNA she's carrying!" Nadine shot back.

"She's not carrying DNA. That was Ed's way of getting her involved. She's free to go."

Rosa glanced at Nadine. Ed had dragged her into this by suggesting that she had the DNA Saytir needed.

"Is it true?" she mumbled, feeling her anger flaring.

"It's true. We have all the DNA we need. The kid that was killed in L.A.? C-Force had our people there. We took samples. But let's be serious. The cops are chasing you and you have nowhere to go. Sooner or later they will catch you. Come home. History is being made tonight. The ChupaCabra and the Roswell alien genomes are complete. We can proceed to—how shall I say—creation. You have to see this."

"You're sick, Saytir. C-Force has done a job on you."

"I am not sick!" Saytir exploded. "This is science! And C-Force is with us."

"To create monsters. You know what happened the last time. You can dress the clones in human skin, but they're still monsters. No heart. Automatons!"

"That was an early experiment! You know that! Now we have the real thing! We have the DNA of the lost colony of our . . . of our ancestors, the original ChupaCabras. We're bringing them back to life. A deviant strain. Others are taking DNA from the marrow of a Neanderthal's bones, and sooner or later they will clone him! We're just ahead of the game! We have ChupaCabra and alien DNA! We have the genomes! And the combination will be powerful! A new life-form!"

Nadine hesitated. They were approaching the sprawling industrial park. She pointed at the brightly lit building, Saytir's lab, and Rosa drove up to the gate.

"Okay, Saytir, you win. I'll come home. But you have to assure me Rosa will be safe."

"I give my word."

"How can I be sure?"

"I can see the car from where I stand. I've called off the guards. Tell your friend to drive away. She will be safe."

Rosa parked the car and looked at Nadine. At the door of the building loomed a shadow. Saytir.

"Just me," Nadine said.

"Yes, just you. You know that's the way it was meant to be—"

Nadine offed the phone. She leaned back in the seat and closed her eyes.

Rosa waited.

"End of the road," Nadine said.

Rosa nodded. Saytir's lab. A celebration going on inside, and Saytir waiting at the entrance.

"We can both drive away," Rosa pleaded. "We can go to authorities. They can help. The FBI. Anyone. Expose everything!"

Nadine shook her head. "The conspiracy is too deep in the government. It's too late. Look at himit. Gloating it over humanity. Ready to mix the DNA, ready to create the monsters of the future."

"There's still time," Rosa said, but she already knew. The puzzle, Ed's plan, had fallen into place.

Nadine turned to Rosa. "I am not what I am," she whispered.

"I know," Rosa replied.

"You knew? Why did you stay?"

"Friendship, I guess. I began to understand I could help."

Nadine reached across and touched Rosa's hand. "The only friends I ever had were Ed and Marcy. Now you. We don't know friendship, can't feel it. You can. You and Ed, you're good people. I am lucky to have known you."

"I am lucky to have known you. Eve."

Nadine smiled. "Yes, I guess I had something of Eve in me. I am that rebellious clone. The sheit they couldn't control." She paused and laughed softly. "I wish things had worked out. Ed tried to make me human. All those books and music, movies, conversations about emotions . . ."

"He did a good job."

Nadine shrugged. "Thank you for being a friend. For understanding. But this is the end of the line. Get out."

Rosa hesitated. She thought of protesting, but she knew this is how it had to be. There was no turning back. She opened the door and stepped out.

Nadine slid into the driver's seat. "By the way, did you know Ed's mother lives in Santa Rosa?"

"No."

"Just up the road if you decide to visit her someday. She doesn't know Ed is dead. Won't know unless you—I don't want to burden you. You've done so much. But in the future if you decide to see her . . . here's her address."

She handed Rosa a piece of paper. "Good-bye Rosa. Thanks for everything."

"Good-bye, Nadine. I wish you didn't have to—"

"Gotta do it, girl. Ed's plan. Down with C-Force!" She shouted a long and loud, "Aaaaa-jua!"

Rosa stepped back and Nadine gunned the car toward the building. A confident Saytir stood at the front door, illuminated by the bright lights. Nadine, the only female of the first cloning experiments, was coming home.

Himit smiled as the car jumped forward, but the look turned into one of disbelief, then terror.

"No!" Saytir cried and turned to run, but it was too late. The car smashed into himit, plunging Saytir into the lab and the horrendous explosion that followed. The entire building went up in a mushroom cloud, a towering inferno that lit up the sky.

The blast sent Rosa toppling to the ground. The accompanying shock wave broke windows all over Roswell.

CHAPTER 24

"You okay, lady?"

"What the hell was she doing out here?"

"Beats me. Lady? You okay? We called an ambulance."

Rosa opened her eyes and in the soft, violet light of dawn tried to focus on the face hanging over her. A policeman.

Clones, she thought. What can I . . . kick him, run? Nadine is dead . . . the fire . . . she looked at the flames and curling smoke. Around her a hubbub of noise, police sirens, officers barking orders through megaphones, men running in the fire trucks' swirling red lights.

Rosa grew aware she was lying on the ground. A black policeman held her hand. His hand was warm; he smiled.

"I'm okay . . ." She struggled to sit up.

"Stay still, lady. Paramedics will be here any minute. You're lucky we found you. You could've been run over."

"What were you doing out here?" the second cop asked. His tone harsh.

Rosa's mind cleared. Nadine had driven the car with the explosives into the lab. A terrible explosion. She remembered being lifted off the ground and then falling to earth.

She looked at the two policemen. City cops? Or himits? They could mean trouble. Were they friendly or some of Saytir's clones still roaming the earth? She had to think straight. What was she doing here?

"Jogging."

"Jogging?"

"Yes, I get up early and jog . . ." She pushed the policeman's arm aside and sat up. "There was a fire . . . I guess I fell."

"An explosion lady. The whole complex is gone. Went up in flames."

"What was it?" Rosa asked.

"A building. Part of the gated complex out here. Secret stuff."

"You sure you can sit? The medics will be here any minute."

"We don't know what was in the building. But whatever it was must have been important."

"Army sent troops in to cordon off the area. I swear, those choppers were here in no time. They won't let us near. They even want our fire trucks outta here. Whole thing is going to burn to the ground."

Rosa looked again toward the fire. Her vision had cleared and she could see men in dark military uniforms, bayonets drawn, surrounding the burning building. Overhead, helicopters buzzed back and forth, landing at the old airstrip to drop off more troops.

"Soldiers?"

"Not just soldiers, C-Force SWAT teams. These guys mean business. Told us to go home, they're running the show. Told the chief not to report the fire. Must be military."

"Just like '47," one said. "My dad was here. He said the road from here to Corona was sealed off. They were boxing stuff and taking it to Alamogordo. The newspaper said a UFO had crashed. Remember?"

"How can I forget," the cop near Rosa said. "First they said they had found a space alien. Did the famous autopsy. I saw the video on the Internet. Then the army came in and clamped down. Made the paper retract its story. Sealed off Roswell. Info had to go out through military channels. Enough to make a believer out of you."

"Ah, just baloney," the other cop said and helped Rosa to her feet. "You sure you're okay? We should have you checked out."

Rosa looked at him. Not a clone. Nadine had said she could hear the clones make a buzzing sound. Rosa heard nothing. These were real cops just doing their work.

"Are you real?"

The policeman chuckled. "Yes, I'm real."

They were interrupted by a heavyset C-Force officer who came striding up. "Hey, why haven't you two moved out? You have orders to clear out!"

"Yes sir, we do," the cop answered. "But we couldn't leave this woman here—"

The officer pushed him aside and looked at Rosa. His face was square, stern, reminding Rosa of Saytir. His stare penetrated, chilling Rosa.

"What the hell are you doing here?" he asked.

"She was jogging—" the cop answered, but the C-Force officer cut him off.

"I'm asking her! What were you doing here?"

Rosa had the sudden premonition that if she got arrested by C-Force, she would never be heard from again. Whatever clones were left of the conspiracy that Ed and Nadine had destroyed would recognize her. She could trust no one.

"I jog here every morning—"

"What did you see?" he asked, butting his face against hers, creating a slight vibrating sensation in Marcy's bracelet. Marcy was saying be strong, don't show fear, fight back.

"I didn't see anything," Rosa replied, gathering courage to look him in the eyes. "Suddenly there was an explosion and I tripped—"

"Did you see anyone? A vehicle, people, anything?"

"No, nothing. It was still dark, so I was paying attention to the path—"

The officer glared at her. He was on the verge of arresting her when one of the cops interrupted.

"She jogs here every morning, just like a lot of other folks."

The C-Force officer turned and spat. "Get her out of here! And you boys clear out too! We have a terrorist plot on our hands!" With that he turned and stomped away.

"Terrorist plot baloney," the cop whispered.

"You better come with us," his partner said. "Not safe here. You have a car?"

"No. My husband drops me off on his way to work," Rosa lied.

"We can drop you wherever you want."

"Thanks. I have to meet a friend downtown."

"No problem. That C-Force joker treats us like kids. So let him take over. Whatever they're hiding is none of our business." He opened the car door for Rosa.

She paused to look at the fire, dying now as it burned itself out. She thought of Nadine and Ed. Their ending was tragic, but appropriate. They had planned it that way. Destroy Saytir's evil project.

But it wasn't just Saytir's plan. C-Force was a wider conspiracy. The government was involved, and it had the money to buy all the scientists it needed. It controlled the SWAT team that had just moved in to secure the area. What else did it control? How far did its tentacles extend?

The thoughts troubled Rosa as she sat in the back seat of the police cruiser heading toward downtown Roswell.

C-Force had found the first ChupaCabras in the mountains of Puerto Rico and cloned the beasts. Beasts? Maybe the ChupaCabras weren't monsters. Just another lost colony in the human evolutionary scheme. Was it possible? Were there colonies of hominids hiding away in impenetrable jungles and inaccessible mountaintops? Had evolution created different humanlike species? If the

Neanderthal was possible, why not others? Lost ancestors. Some disappeared. Some still in hiding.

Rosa shivered. The genome computer files C-Force created were lost in the fire. Did they have backup copies? Was Saytir so sure of his power that he would not have allowed copies? I have a copy, she said to herself, and touched the CD in her pocket.

But C-Force was not done yet. One thing was true of the world: that when men desired the power of gods, they would stop at nothing to get it.

"Where can we leave you?" the officer asked, looking at her.

"Can you drop me off in front of the UFO museum?"

The officer shrugged. "No problem. You sure you don't feel dizzy or anything like that?"

"I feel fine," Rosa replied.

They pulled up in front of the museum and the officer jumped out and opened Rosa's door. "About time for breakfast," he said as Rosa alighted.

"Yes," Rosa replied, aware of people on the street.

"Well, good luck. You'll have a story to tell your grandkids. You were there when that building exploded. Who knows, maybe they were doing alien autopsies in there."

He and his partner laughed. Rosa smiled. "Thanks. You've been very kind."

"No problem, lady. That's what we're here for."

The car drove off. Rosa looked around her. The sun had risen, bathing everything in startling spring light. In the background sirens still sounded, and the column of black smoke was still visible.

Best to get out of town, thought Rosa, looking around her. On the streets people were going about their business. The day's gossip would be about the big fire at the industrial park.

For Rosa it had been a long night. A night she would never forget.

CHAPTER 25

Rosa walked to the bus station and checked the bus schedule. A bus left for Santa Rosa in an hour. She found a pay phone and called her parents.

"Hija, thank God you called," her mother answered. "Are you in Roswell? We worried about you. It's in the news, a big explosion. Did you see it? Are you all right? And Nadine?"

Rosa reassured her mother that she was fine. She was not near the explosion. Lying again, but there was no need to worry her parents. What she had been through would take time to explain.

"I want to go by Santa Rosa and visit Ed's mother."

"Ed's mother? Nadine's uncle. How thoughtful of you, Rosa. I'm sure she will appreciate a visit. My grandfather was raised in Puerto de Luna. He knew the Lopez family, the Cordovas, los Chavez, Candelarias . . . all of them. We used to visit when I was a girl. What is Ed's family name?"

Rosa didn't know, but she would find out. And yes, she would try to skip down to Puerto de Luna. Her mother had assumed she was still with Nadine.

When she hung up she called Bobby. He wasn't in, so she left a voice message. There was a lot to talk about, later, when there was time.

Lots of time, she thought. Together. She needed to talk about what had happened, try to make sense of it.

After she hung up, she went to the ticket counter and bought a one-way ticket to Santa Rosa, then went to the bathroom to clean up. She felt drained, physically and emotionally. Bone tired. You can sleep on the bus, she told herself.

But why not go straight home? She looked in the mirror. Her face showed the exhaustion of the night. Because she owed it to Ed. Deliver the sad news. The dead deserve that. One must give notice when a friend dies.

In this case there was little to do except support Ed's mother. There was no body to bury, no remains, but the woman had to know her son had died a hero. She would never know the entire story, but Rosa would tell her the heroic part. Were it not for Ed, Nadine, and Marcy, in a few years the world would have seen a far greater danger than global warming: the rule by a government that controlled with the monsters it created. Not science fiction, but reality.

Rosa bought a bean burrito, an apple, and coffee. She hurried aboard the bus and found a seat across the aisle from a woman and her young daughter. Rosa greeted the woman, who responded in Spanish.

"I speak English," she explained as the bus left the station and headed north on 285. "Vamos a Denver," the woman continued. "I am Amada, and this is my daughter, María Teresa."

"Mucho gusto. Me llamo Rosa—"

"I speak English too," María chipped in. "I went to primary."

"A Mennonite teacher came," the mother explained. "Muy bonita. Now children in our village speak the inglés."

"Very good," Rosa said. "Would you like an apple?" She handed María the apple.

María looked at her mother for consent and Amada nodded. "Muchas gracias," she said and took the apple.

Amada was eager to talk, telling Rosa that she and her daughter were going to meet her husband who worked in Denver. He worked hard for a paint company and had become foreman of a crew. Many people from Chihuahua had migrated to el norte looking for work, she explained. The family had been separated for three years, so they were very excited about the reunion and their new life in el norte.

"But we have no papers," she whispered in the end. "I am afraid. We pay mucho dinero to cross la frontera. The coyotes cost many dollars. They tell us, take bus at El Paso y adiós. Is the boleto good?"

She handed Rosa her bus tickets.

"Yes, it's good. You will go to Alburquerque and change to a bus going to Denver. It's correct."

"Gracias a Dios. Thank you, Rosa. I bother you—"

"No, not at all. I am happy to help. Is there anything else I can do?"

She looked into Amada's dark eyes. Something was bothering her. Amada's handsome face was drawn with concern.

"There is a story," she said and waited. "I have to tell you. I know."

Rosa nodded. "Yes, go on."

Amada began her story. "We lived in a village south of Casas Grandes. Very poor. Near the sierra. Isolated. Before my husband went to el norte he grew corn. I had only three goats to care for. One evening I was out late. A star came from the sky. Bright with many colors. I was afraid. I prayed to la Virgen María. I have never been so frightened. The sky was on fire. But the lights of the star were so beautiful. It was like magic.

"It was not a star. It was a boat that came from the sky. There were people inside. Not like us, but they moved. How do I know?

They took me up into their ship. I swear by the saints they took me inside!

"Do you understand?" her plea cried out to be believed.

"Yes. I understand," Rosa replied, thinking of Marcy. It seemed so much time had passed, and yet it was only last night that the rose ship had taken her. Ships, boats, flying objects, the Argonauts of space, the brethren, lowriders, primos—whatever they were called, they came to visit.

And now here was another story of one of those extraterrestrial ships from the heavens landing near a village at the foothills of the Sierra Madre.

What could she say? No, I don't believe. Maybe Marcy just disappeared into the desert. Yes, that's how it happened. Some kind of hypnosis. Or getting into a flying saucer was simply a metaphor for death. The brain loved metaphors. Ascending to be with God, or gods. The resurrection promised. A kind of personal rapture promised by many religions. Someone died and grief created a kind of hysteria. Made believers out of nonbelievers.

Rosa leaned over and held the woman's hand. What could she say? I had a friend who last night went up in such a rose-colored UFO. I mean a ship. A boat. A coffin.

"You were alone?"

"Yes."

"Go on," Rosa said. She felt Amada's story was not yet done.

"When they returned me to earth I went home. I took my goats home, as if nothing happened. Of course, I felt like I had died.

"Then the strange things begin. The following day I went to the market. The women were talking, but I could hear what they were thinking. Yes, I could hear their thoughts. I had acquired a gift! But when I told them their thoughts they grew angry. I told the women what they were thinking. I thought it was a miracle.

"But no. They did not like to have their thoughts known. I didn't realize I was exposing their intimate desires. I began to know who they really were and what they believed. So many of the thoughts were petty, full of envy, greed, jealousies, desires, needs, and deceptions. At the core, in their souls, my neighbors were frail. Their words were pleasant, but many of their thoughts were poison.

"The women began to stay away from me. They said I was a witch. They said I was evil for exposing the truth in their souls. I could no longer go to the market. I could not go to church, for even the priest had evil thoughts. No one would buy my husband's corn. We became outcasts in our own village.

"That is why he came to el norte. At first I thought he had deserted me and my daughter. You see, I had never told him I had been aboard that sky ship. He suspected something, but said nothing. His thoughts remained pure. But he left, and for three years I was like a widow.

"Then just last week he wrote to me. He sent money. He wants us to live with him as we did before. He wants to see his daughter. I am so happy. So we start a new life. But there is a warning. Never wish to go up in those ships from the heavens. We do not know those people. They are so advanced. They have such great powers. We humans are not ready for such powers."

Then she grew silent.

After a few moments had passed Rosa spoke. "Thank you for telling me your story. You have been through a lot. But, if I may ask you: why did you choose me to tell your story?" Rosa glanced around. There were other Mexican women on the bus, some traveling with husbands and families, and yet Amada had been drawn to her. María had sat silent during the telling. The little girl knew of her mother's experience.

Amada too glanced around, then whispered. "You wear the bracelet."

Rosa looked at Marcy's bracelet.

"You wear the bracelet," Amada repeated, and pulled up her sleeve to reveal an identical bracelet.

"When I came back from the sky ship," she explained, "I was wearing this. They gave it to me. Now I have to tell my story to those who wear such bracelets. Do you understand?"

CHAPTER 26

The bus pulled up in front of the bus stop, a small gas station on the west side of Santa Rosa.

"I get off here," Rosa told Amada, "so I have to say good-bye. Adios y buena suerte."

Amada reached for her hand. Rosa felt a warm vibration. Whatever power the bracelet conveyed, it was certainly in this woman going north to start a new life.

"You are strong, Rosa. Many things will happen to you, but you will survive and grow stronger. You will be rich. Not with money, but in your soul."

"You are courageous," Rosa replied, "to start a new life in a country you do not know. But it will be good for you and María."

"Yes. I am positive," Amada replied. "A new life. Que Dios te bendiga."

"Gracias." Rosa turned to go.

"Thank you for the apple," María called.

"De nada. Be good." She waved, got off the bus, and walked into the gas station.

She had just stepped through the door when someone called her name. "Rosa!"

Rosa looked at the dark, attractive woman approaching her. Dressed in a colorful skirt, Navajo blouse, and a turquoise necklace as accent, her long black hair flowing, she drew the attention of the men in the lobby.

"Amy Cordova!" Rosa exclaimed as Amy gathered her in an embrace.

"What are you doing in Santa Rosa?" both asked at the same time.

"Wow! What a coincidence. I brought some of my paintings to show at the library," Amy said. "I'm on my way back to Taos. Stopped for gas. And you?"

"I'm visiting a friend," Rosa said.

"Anyone I know?"

"Do you remember Ed from high school?"

"Ed. Yeah. He was really good at science. You came to see him?"

"His mother. Ed died recently . . ."

"Oh, I'm sorry. Lo siento. Had you kept up with him?"

"Not really, but his mother lives in town. She lives by the lake."

"A lovely place. So tranquil. I went to see the Sonny Rivera statue. Have you seen it?"

"No. I haven't been here in years."

"You have to see it. I sat there and contemplated about art and its place in our lives. I gave a talk at the library last night. I was going to talk about my work, and I did, but I found myself drifting into the role of creativity. Our work is our spirituality. It comes from our ancestors, los viejitos. And its all around us, right here. I feel it. If I didn't have my gallery in Taos, I'd start one here."

"My mother is from Puerto de Luna," Rosa replied. "I know what you mean about the ambience."

"But you came on the bus. Do you have a car? Are you meeting someone?"

"I was going to walk—"

"Walk? Come on. I'll drive you. It is so good to see you, mujer. Tell me what you've been up to. I read about the L.A. thing. Is it true, you tackled a ChupaCabra? Hijo! I'm so proud of you."

As they drove toward Park Lake Rosa talked about her teaching and a few details of the cruise ship adventure. Amy listened intently.

"And all I've been doing is painting. You lead an adventurous life, Rosa."

Adventure, thought Rosa. All I ever wanted to do was to teach. I didn't ask for adventure, and yet these past few months have been a roller coaster. What if I told Amy what really happened last night? Would she believe me?

"Come to Taos; see my gallery. Stay with me. We need to catch up—is this the house?"

"That's the address I have. Lake Drive."

A woman sat on the porch. Ed's mother, Rosa guessed.

"I won't go in. Do you need a ride after you see her?"

"No, you go on. I plan to stay the night."

"Okay. Sorry about Ed. The bracelet. Where did you get it?"

"A gift."

"It's exquisite. I saw one in Taos. A woman from the pueblo . . . anyway, come and see me, I mean it. Call me."

She pressed one of her cards into Rosa's hand and kissed her cheek. "I really want to see you. There are strange things happening in Taos. Paranormal stuff. Strange lights at night. Right over the gorge. And they saw a ChupaCabra in Peñasco. Is it coming north? Used to be la Llorona at the river, now kids claim they've seen a ChupaCabra. Serves them right if they're doing dope. I don't know what to believe. Can you come?"

"I promise," Rosa replied. "It's good to see you. I'll call you."

She stepped out of the car, waved, and Amy waved and drove away. Rosa turned to greet the woman on the porch.

The woman rose to greet her. Attractive, in her late forties Rosa guessed, with a resemblance to the Ed she remembered. Ed had been a handsome guy

"I'm Ana, Ed's mother," she said, looking into Rosa's eyes. "He's dead, isn't he?"

Rosa nodded.

"I felt it," Ana said, her eyes filling with tears. She turned and looked at the lake. "He grew up here. Spent summers collecting arrowheads in the hills, wandering along the river . . . he would come home with his pockets full of frogs, insects, plants, rocks . . . he saw a world most of us never see. Always alone . . ."

"I'm sorry," Rosa whispered.

"You look tired," Ana said. "You need to rest. Let's go in. You take a shower; I'll get you a pair of pajamas. You need to eat. Something light, some atole. Then you can rest. There will be time to talk later."

Rosa stood in the hot shower, letting the water drain away the sweat and fatigue of the night. She dressed in the pajamas and entered the kitchen. Ana served her the hot cereal.

"Ed used to love atole. Simple food is best, he used to say. I don't know where he got all his ideas. Sometimes our own children are born with a connection to some power bigger than us. This place helped. He loved it here. This is Eden, he used to say. Sun Lines run through here. That's why legends could be reborn here." She paused. "I'm talking too much. Get to bed. We can visit later."

Rosa fell asleep the minute her head hit the pillow. An exhausted sleep full of images: rose windows, faces, a fire engulfing the world, a gold fish as big as the earth giving birth to humans that swam like fish, dozens of images, and then darkness.

When she awoke, the afternoon shadows had descended. She dressed, hurried out, and found Ana sitting in the porch.

"You look rested. Are you hungry?"

"No. A few dreams, then I slept like a log. I feel refreshed. Thank you so much."

"No, thank you, Rosa. Thank you for coming. And for being there for Ed. Would you like to walk by the lake? The wind is so still. The kids are gone. This, and early morning, are my favorite times to walk there. Who knows, we might even see the Golden Carp."

Ana smiled, took Rosa's arm, and together they crossed the street. The lake was calm, its waters a golden sheet reflecting the light of the western sun.

The lake and the little river and the hills beyond all reflected the golden hue that had settled over the land. In the background the town went about its business, but at the lake a holy hush had descended.

As they walked around the lake Rosa told Ana about Roswell.

"It's what he had to do," Ana said, accepting the death of her son.

She pointed. "This is where he roamed as a child, along the river. He swam in the lake, the Blue Hole, el Rito . . . always looking for the Golden Carp. Even as a child he taught me there is beauty in nature. The legend of the Golden Carp is more than just a story, he said. God is in the fish, in the water, the hills, the rocks, in every-thing. Imagine, he was a child and already knew so much of the mystery and beauty of this place."

"You moved to Santa Fe . . ."

"Yes. His father died and I had family there. It wasn't easy for Ed, but we survived. Years later I moved back here. He got his degree and was working, but he was here every weekend. Still tramping up and down the river. As far as Puerto de Luna. In the hills."

They sat and enjoyed the beauty of the lake. A family was start-ing a picnic at one of the grills. Books in hand, a few tourists had paused in front of the Rivera statue.

"His life served a purpose," Rosa said.

"Yes," Ed's mother agreed. "For that I give thanks. His life had meaning."

A breeze danced across the lake, a fish jumped, creating a circle of ripples. Something wondrous and beautiful was stirring in the water and the surrounding landscape.

As they talked, the light of the spring day fled west, leaving the colors of a divine palette splashed on the huge clouds that had risen. Later, a full moon would rise and be reflected on the lake's surface, the same waters in which swam the Golden Carp.

AUTHOR'S NOTE

Literature and movies are full of stories dealing with science gone wild. As a teenager I remember being fascinated by one of the early Frankenstein movies. Today there are rapid advances in DNA and stem-cell research, which inspired me to write this story. I asked myself: what if DNA technology goes Frankenstein? What if the same science that is being used to cure so many diseases is used for evil purposes?

History teaches us that science has been of great benefit to humanity. I hope this story encourages the young to learn more about science. The future depends on young people who are knowledgeable both in science and the humanities.

Future generations must deal with the complicated questions raised by scientific inquiry. As science probes deeper into the life-force and the essence of what makes us human, society must also deal with the ethical questions generated by such advancements.